PLANET OF WAR!

"You seem to be surviving very well," Starbuck said, "for children."

"We are not children!" Kyle shouted.

"What are you then, all you eight and ten and fourteen year olds, if you're not children?"

"We are warriors!"

THE YOUNG WARRIORS

The newest BATTLESTAR GALACTICA adventure

Berkley Battlestar Galactica Books

BATTLESTAR GALACTICA
by Glen A. Larson and Robert Thurston

BATTLESTAR GALACTICA 2: THE CYLON DEATH MACHINE
by Glen A. Larson and Robert Thurston

BATTLESTAR GALACTICA 3: THE TOMBS OF KOBOL
by Glen A. Larson and Robert Thurston

BATTLESTAR GALACTICA 4: THE YOUNG WARRIORS
by Glen A. Larson and Robert Thurston

BATTLESTAR GALACTICA: THE PHOTOSTORY
by Glen A. Larson; Edited and Adapted by Richard J. Anobile

BattlestaR
GALACTICA 4
THE YOUNG WARRIORS

NOVEL BY GLEN A. LARSON
AND ROBERT THURSTON

Based on the Universal Television Series
BATTLESTAR GALACTICA
Created by
GLEN A. LARSON
Adapted from the episode
"THE YOUNG WARRIORS"
Teleplay by Donald Bellisario,
Frank Lupo & Paul Playdon

Teleplay by DONALD BELLISARIO,
FRANK LUPO & PAUL PLAYDON

BERKLEY BOOKS, NEW YORK

BATTLESTAR GALACTICA 4:
THE YOUNG WARRIORS

A Berkley Book / published by arrangement with
MCA PUBLISHING, a Division of MCA Inc.

PRINTING HISTORY
Berkley edition / August 1980

ISBN: 0-425-04655-9

A BERKLEY BOOK ® TM 757,375
Berkley Books are published by Berkley Publishing Corporation,
200 Madison Avenue, New York, New York 10016.
PRINTED IN THE UNITED STATES OF AMERICA

CHAPTER ONE

The report from Core Central Records showed that the *Galactica*'s therapy rooms had not serviced anyone in a long, long time. When he first read the information he had requested about therapy, Lieutenant Starbuck had been astonished that *nobody* had been troubled enough to seek therapy lately, especially considering all the agonies the crew of the ship had experienced since the Cylon ambush had wiped out most of human civilization on the twelve worlds. On the other hand, perhaps the neglect of the therapy rooms was not so surprising. After all, everyone had been so busy either running the ship or fighting battles with Cylon attackers—who had time for treatment of comparatively trivial psychological problems? Well, right now Starbuck did, and he intended to use it.

His information printout showed that some time ago a memo had been sent out by a subcommittee of the Council of the Twelve which had suggested closing down the therapy rooms and converting their extensive equipment to some more useful activity. However, the medical staff had apparently been too busy to act on the memo's recommendations. *Well,* Starbuck thought, *I can rationalize my therapy session, call it an inspection of the facility's resources, make a few recommendations myself. Now that's really scarey. I'm beginning to think like an intership memo. I may need more help than I thought!*

He found the therapy rooms off a dark corridor that did not seem to be used by any crewmembers. Walking along it gave Starbuck eerie feelings. There were no dark

1

corridors anywhere else in the *Galactica*. In fact, the
only time he'd traveled through dismal poorly lit passages like this one had been on his only visit to the prison
ship, sometimes known as the grid barge, on a special
mission. Those corridors at least had a few complaining
prisoners to break up the spooky silence.

The door to the first therapy room was slightly ajar.
A shiver went up Starbuck's spine just before he nudged
it open. He went into the room tentatively, ready to
spring back to the dark corridor if he found anything
unexpected inside. If anyone caught him in the room,
he fully intended to use his inspection excuse and pretend
he had no intention of seeking therapy. The room lights
went on as soon as Starbuck stepped through the doorway. There must be sensors implanted in the door frame,
he thought. The room was bare, its sole article of furniture a velvet-surfaced blue couch. There were several
small square compartments lined in short rows on all
four gray walls. Starbuck had seen such compartments
before, in some of the recreational cubicles on the ship's
rest areas. The compartments contained fantasy-interplay
devices, derived from Sagitaran technology, which could
create, control, and embellish on fantasies requested by
the person using them. Starbuck had not known that
therapy rooms made use of fantasy-interplay technology.

Just being here is my own fantasy, Starbuck thought.
*Silly, really. I don't need psychological help. Here I am
a hero of the fleet, skypilot deluxe, with so many medals
they'd twist my chest out of shape if I actually wore all
of them. Heroes don't need therapy. It's in the manuals—
heroes are stable, forthright fellows. So what if I'm losing a little sleep? A little sleep! Can't remember when
I last nodded off. So what if I'm not my usual cheerful
self? Who needs cheerful? I haven't felt cheerful since
we left Kobol. Hard to feel the least bit up when the
commander is solemnly going around mourning the fact
that he didn't leave Kobol with the knowledge of where
his precious fabled Earth was located. So what if I feel*

like I'm going to shatter into pieces like an exploding Cylon raider at any moment? So what if my own ship feels like a stranger? And a hostile stranger at that. It's only a phase. I'll get over it. I don't need therapy. I should just turn right around and—

"Lie down, please," said a gentle voice that seemed, in spite of its softness, to fill the room. Like a command whisper, or an urgent muttering from Commander Adama, it demanded obeisance. Starbuck could not see any speakers in the usual places along the wall. The voice must come out of the vents that surrounded the blue velvet couch. "Lie down, please," the voice said again, in just the same way it had spoken before, with no change in pitch, timbre, or inflection. Starbuck knew he should obey the voice, and lie down, but it was his nature to resist even a hint of authority.

"Couldn't I just stand?" Starbuck asked. "Anyway, I'm not even sure I need to be here."

"All my clients are not sure they belong here," the voice said. "When you came through the door you'd already made the decision to seek help. That is good. I am happy that you have come to that decision. But, in order for me to be fully functional, it is necessary that you lie down on the—"

"Did I hear right? You're happy I'm here? How can you be *happy*? You're just a device, a programmed construct of wires, circuits, and—"

"It is necessary that you—"

"All right, all right. I get it, I'll lie down."

The couch was surprisingly comfortable, so soft and luxuriant that Starbuck seemed to float on its velvet surface like a swimmer on the lazy waves of a salty Caprican lake. Maybe this was all he needed. A good rest. Maybe, after all, it was just his bunk that was causing his sleeplessness. An old standard-issue mattress and not psychological difficulties at all. He felt as if he could drop off to sleep immediately. But if he did he might then encounter one of the nightmares that had come during the rare times when he had slept.

"Specify your problem, please," the voice said.

"Well, it's not that easy to—"

"Of course not. Just try to put it as simply as possible. I have many programs in my storage banks, many therapies at my beck and call. As you speak, I will be narrowing down the perimeters of your treatment, selecting the therapy that may work best for you. But you must explain your problem. In detail. Just put it in your own words."

Starbuck suspected that sensors within the couch were scanning his body for physical clues. A compilation of data about his blood pressure, temperature, the state of his nerves, and any minor physical ailments would, he knew, contribute to the successful operation of the therapy room mechanisms.

"I don't know where to start."

"Patients usually have that problem at the beginning."

"Patients? Hey, I'm not a patient, I'm just here to—"

"Of course. I will not use that word again."

Starbuck thought he heard a click. The device had probably entered the information, do not use the word *patient* with this patient. This therapy routine was too pat, too systematized, it couldn't possibly help him. Well, he'd started all this, might as well go through with it.

"All right. Why I'm here. It's got to do with what I do, my duties in a way."

"Ah, a job-related identity crisis. Good. And your job is?"

A certain smugness in the voice was beginning to irritate Starbuck. Anyway, who could feel confident, or even friendly, toward a machine that said *Ah*?

"I'm a viper pilot. A warrior. I fly out of this rattletrap and perform missions, fight battles against the Cylons, reconnaissance patrols—"

"Ah, the Cylons are still the enemy."

"Sure they're still the enemy. Where have you been?

They've been the enemy for something like a thousand years. Why should that change?"

There was a pause, and the voice actually sounded embarrassed when it replied:

"I have been cut off from the central ship computers and consequently lack certain data. The theory of my programmers is that my functions are best accomplished if I am not confused by knowing the entire context of the ship's situation. An overload of information could interfere with my diagnostic procedures. I must make decisions for *you* and not according to what is best for the Colonial Fleet."

"The Colonial Fleet doesn't even exist any more. It was ambushed, a massive sneak attack by those Cylon creeps."

"You see? It has been a long time since I've been consulted about anything. The war is over?"

"No, not exactly. We're, well, we're fleeing from the enemy, looking for Earth, fighting when we can, stopping for—"

"Earth?"

Starbuck sighed.

"This is hopeless. How can we even communicate? Never mind Earth. I think I better get out of here."

"Specify your problem, please. What trouble are you having with your job?"

"Well, no trouble with the job as such. At least not with doing it. It's, well, it's hard to explain. I just feel frustrated."

"Ah, frustrated. Good. What frustrates you?"

Starbuck squirmed. He'd never liked being interrogated, especially by a voice that he knew was not human. Strange, how often he wound up being asked difficult probing questions by machines. Not long ago, when he had been captured by Cylons and imprisoned on the traitor Baltar's base ship, a bizarre but nevertheless charming walking computer named Lucifer had subjected the young lieutenant to a battery of questions that had nearly shaken the cool Starbuck's self-control. Memories of that encounter with Lucifer still made him uneasy. He stroked the velvet surface of the couch nervously as he tried to answer the therapy room voice.

"It's the war really. At least I think it is. It seems like I've known nothing else but war all my life. When I was a kid, most of my games were war games, most of my playmates were young warriors, or warriors-to-be. My life now is like one of our games—but blown up a thousand times in scale. Even my family kept recalling the war to me. You see, they were disabled veterans, the folks who took care of me. They—"

"The folks who took care of you? Are you referring to your parents?"

"No. They were like a mom and dad, but they weren't really my parents. I was left an orphan, or at least most probably an orphan, by a Cylon attack on my home city. In those days orphans were legally considered victims of the war—see how war plays a part in *every* detail of my life? I can hardly speak of myself or my life without bringing war into it somehow. Anyway, I was classified as victim and was assigned to a pair of other victims for bringing up. It was astonishing how many of my playmates were in the same situation. And those who had genuine parents, they only saw them once in a while. Most adults seemed to be either warriors who were away for long periods, or they were in some important and busy way connected with the war effort. I mean, the war's been going on for so many generations that kids grow up not having an alternative to the idea of war. What alternative could they have? What is peace really, or the idea of peace? Not really the opposite of war, at least not in my experience. Peace is, well, just an abstraction that's supposed to be the opposite of something real, you see? War and peace don't seem to me like legitimate opposites. Anyway, even the businesses not directly connected to the war were essentially governed by the war. They were controlled by rationing and supply quotas, all the terrible business complications that a war brings. The war's everywhere, don't you see? You can't escape from it. Maybe that's my problem really. I just want a minute to myself."

"Hmmm, I see."

Starbuck did not feel comfortable with a machine that hmmmed as well as ahhed.

"So—your parents were killed in that Cylon attack?"

"Presumably. Nobody was ever able to tell me for sure. My father had achieved some notoriety as a gambler, and in the years since I've heard odd rumors of him roaming several worlds and getting into scrapes by taking chances on anything that came his way. But I doubt he's alive. Those are just tall tales, I think."

"Alive or not, the pertinent fact is that you seemed to have lacked parental guidance in your formative years."

"In a way. My foster parents were nice and all. But Gawr, my father had a hook for a hand and he limped— one leg shorter than the other, war injury. My mother, Doreen, had been injured in a laser attack and she'd miraculously survived, but she was nearly blind. Still, they treated me well, normally, like any—"

"But they were not your parents. Go on."

"Okay. So, the war influenced every phase of my life. When I reached the age of career-selection, it seemed only natural to apply for the Flight Academy and train to be a fighter pilot. I'd never really wanted anything else. I was accepted and took to flying a viper by the seat of my pants. I finished top of the class, at least at war and flying skills. My academics weren't all that great, but I got by. After graduation I came to the *Galactica*, the rawest ensign in the history of the fleet, I think, but somehow I became the crack fighter pilot that I am. I give everybody this line about how I hate duty but I'm really very good at it, really very good at war skills."

Starbuck could not suppress the bitterness that had

come into his voice, and he wondered if the therapy machine made note of tonal fluctuations.

"So you see, I've never really gotten away from the war. Even my diversions, gambling and romance, are primarily escapes from war, and I attend to both concerns with the same tactical efficiency I apply to battle. At present I'm manipulating the affections of two fine young women, Athena and Cassiopeia, and I play them off each other with a keen sense of strategy, and I feel guilty about that, but I still do it. God, I'm so tired of the war, this flight from the Cylons, everything. I want to think in some way that doesn't relate to war. These feelings started obsessing me some time ago, when I flew into an anomaly of space called a void. It was completely empty, this void, completely black, I might have been trapped there forever. Ever since, I've been bothered by what once would have been unimportant. The war, my viper, the meaning of things . . . I don't know who I am any longer. I've been getting depressed regularly, been having trouble sleeping, getting nightmares, questioning—"

"Nightmares? Dreams can be very helpful. Tell me about yours."

"Most of my dreams revolve around the war—what else? Either I'm cruising along, and a Cylon ship appears out of nowhere, lasers firing, and I catch that fabled last laser beam in my teeth—or I'm in a raging battle and I watch the enemy whittle our squadron down, I see my friends Boomer and Apollo both killed, and soon I'm the last viper left, and the Cylons trap me in a pinwheel attack and just before I wake up, I feel my ship exploding around me. I can sometimes feel myself disintegrating into little pieces."

"Hmmm."

"What hmmm? You figure something out from that?"

"Perhaps. Go on."

"Well, that's it. I'm functioning in my job as well as

ever. It's just away from it that I'm having trouble coping."

"Do you still feel satisfied at a job well done?"

"Sure. But, you know, it doesn't have *quite* the same meaning for me. I mean, I know I have to carry on the good fight and I understand clearly why I drag myself into a viper cockpit for mission after mission, and I even still get the same old thrills from victories in battle, but sometimes all these achievements don't add up to much. They seem like just so much melted felgercarb."

"Felgercarb?"

"Ummm. Technical term, don't worry about it. Anyway, short of becoming an ambrosa addict, I didn't know how I was going to work all this out. I read about therapy rooms in an old dusty manual and consulted the ship's computer to find my way here. So, the ball's in your third of the triad court, so to speak. What do you think?"

What am I thinking, asking advice from a bunch of circuits and wires? Starbuck thought.

The machine said nothing for a moment, although he thought he could hear a series of clicks within the walls of the room.

"It is difficult to diagnose from a single session," the voice finally said. "As preliminary comment, I would say that you do seem to have a case of disorientation, or perhaps dissociation, which leads to an identity crisis that is quite normal for a man in your position and in your time of life."

"My time of life? You make me sound like—"

"Your role as a fighter pilot and your feelings as a human being do not exactly mesh, causing the symptoms you have described. At this time you are responding more to your feelings and there is an imbalance in your perception of yourself. It is very possible that we must treat that imbalance, try to place your professional life and your interior life on the same kind of par that had existed before the crisis began. I suggest an imagery session to see if we can further define your problems and arrive at a course of treatment, a workable therapy."

"Imagery session? What in Kobol is that?"

"An adaptation of fantasy-interplay technology which allows you to place your areas of psychological difficulty into perspective by seeing them in different contexts, a displacement through imagery that—"

"Hey, hold up a minute! Fantasy-interplay? Displacement? I came here for help, not to play games. Think I'll check out right—"

"Be calm, lieutenant. These will not be games, as you'll see. Perhaps it would be better to begin the first session immediately."

"We don't have to. I'll come back later, I—"

New clicks echoed all around Starbuck as strange devices began emerging from the walls. Some of these devices looked like long glowing sticks; others appeared to be levers, doorknobs, Ovion cabbages. . . .

"What kind of a madhouse is this?" Starbuck muttered.

"Not a madhouse at all. Quite the contrary."

"Stow that, will you? I don't think I really want to— I'm getting out of here."

But, as steel-studded belts slid out of the velvet couch and embraced him tightly, he found that he could not move.

"This is crazy. Let me go."

"I have chosen animal imagery for you. A very common starting point, lieutenant. I have had significant success with using animal imagery to treat battle fatigue."

"Battle fatigue? I don't have—"

"Let me handle diagnostic matters, please. Listen, you are riding through a forest. Think of a forest, see a forest."

Trees seemed to form suddenly all around him and, just as suddenly, he was no longer bound. He even realized he was sitting up on the couch, in spite of the fact he could no longer see the couch. He felt free, even exuberant, riding along through a very green dense forest. Red, purple, and blue flowers lined the riding path.

"Your animal, lieutenant. Think of the animal you are riding on, see it."

Immediately the animal began to take shape. It was a strongly-muscled horse, a black horse with a white mane, galloping along rapidly, fiercely, its nostrils snorting, the suggestion of thin red flames coming out of them.

"A fairly conventional horse image," the voice said. "A handsome strong steed. But so dark in color, lieutenant. Is it your dark thoughts made manifest? Give him a good ride, feel the warm wind!"

Starbuck, who had never been much of a rider—who, in fact, would not even approach a horse except to flirt with a horsewoman—leaned forward like a jockey and urged the black horse forward, patting the amazingly soft hairs of its clean white mane. He lost a clear perspective on the surrounding forest. Colors blended into each other, trees blurred together.

"Watch out ahead, lieutenant."

In front of him, blocking his path, was a red knight on an auburn horse. He held a lance out in front of him, a lance whose sharp point appeared to be speckled with dried blood. The lance was aimed right at Starbuck's throat. Starbuck leaned far to his left and pulled hard on his black steed's reins. The red knight was not able to move his lance quickly enough to aim another blow at Starbuck, who sped past, then gradually eased his horse to a whirling stop.

"What am I supposed to do?"

"Simply respond to the situation. Remember it is not real."

"Respond with what?"

"Any weapon you desire."

The red knight had turned his horse and, head bent, was rushing toward Starbuck, again with his lance held straight out.

"Okay, since it isn't real, let's not fool around here. Give me a laser pistol. Quick!"

The pistol appeared in his hand and, an instant later, he fired it. Its beam seemed to travel along the lance in bright even arcs before penetrating the red knight's chest. The knight fell gracelessly backward, his body striking the ground with a hollow clunking sound. His lance flew into the trees and caught on a branch, sending tremulous vibrations through the leaves. The auburn horse galloped riderless past Starbuck. When the lieutenant turned around to watch its flight, he saw that it had disappeared from the fantasy landscape. Obviously the animal was no longer required for this particular adventure. Looking back to the front, he saw that the red knight was not sprawled on the ground any more, although there was a very realistic plot of scarred ground where the body had been. The lance was still shaking in the tree above him.

"What was that bloody game all about?" Starbuck shouted.

The therapy room voice seemed to emerge from vents in the trunks of several trees:

"You tell me. Interpret your own dream."

"How do you expect me to—wait. These things mean something, right?"

"Perhaps."

"My horse is dark, pitch-black, snorting fire, galloping furiously, carrying me along with a purpose. The blackness and the fire—well, they mean something about the war, don't they? You called them my dark thoughts before. The evil of war, its violence. The red knight— well, the enemy, I suppose. Why red? Wait, I can guess. The Cylons have that stupid red light going back and forth on the rim of their helmets. Red knight, red light. And the red knight appeared suddenly, just the way Cylons seem to, out of ambush. But why a knight? Why not a monster or a real Cylon? Let's work on it. All right, a knight's encased in heavy armor, its reality hidden from the enemy by all that metal. Same with a Cylon. Cylons are a terrifying awesome mystery inside their fighting outfits, underneath those red-light helmets. It's like, well, they're not real, like they're some sort of machines—killing machines that come at you relentlessly, ready to slice you in half without warning. We've never really been able to find out much about Cylons, you know, at least not as a race of sentient beings. When we deal with them directly, they're always masked by the uniforms, and we can't make much out of a dead Cylon. I mean, they're definitely alien, sort of lizardish skin yet on a vaguely insectoid head and a rather humanoid body, but when they're killed more than half their internal organs turn to dust, maybe they even self-destruct, and our medical people have never been able to come to many sensible conclusions about what's left. They've even found a second brain in some Cylons, always in the ugly heads of officers of the elite class, the ones with the dark bands of honor on their uniforms. Anyway, the reason for the knight as imagery for Cylons might simply be the bulky armor hiding the essential humanity of the knight, just as the Cylons' uniform hides an alienness that is equally mystifying for us. Say, am I on a roll, or doesn't any of this make sense?"

"It might. Why do you think you shot your opponent down with a laser pistol rather than battling him on his own terms?"

"Why not? It worked better than a lance or sword, didn't it? Or are you talking some kind of killer instinct? A knight has codes and I don't, is that what you're saying? That his codes make him better than me?"

"I'm saying nothing. I'm not programmed for verbal deception."

"Yeah, you're just a nice straightforward machine. I'd like to kick you in your most sensitive circuits. Okay, so I beamed the knight. I knew he wasn't real anyway, and I gunned him down just to get the charade over with. Nothing wrong with that. No, I'm wrong, there is something. It was callous. I should have at least played out the game, joined the fantasy. But I couldn't. I felt too much anger, something like the hatred I feel for the Cylons when I fire at them. But is that bad? I mean, the Cylon I take out with my pistol or my viper's laser cannon is out to get me, after all. The Cylon forces are out to destroy us, to wipe out the remnants of the human race. We can't have that, can we? Can we?"

"I am not programmed for that sort of moral judgment."

Starbuck sighed.

"Of course not. Neither am I. I'm like you, a machine. Difference is, I'm just programmed to be a functioning war machine. A robot with a laser pistol out to get the enemy constructs whose weapons are aimed at me. That's what's wrong. I really feel that way now. My body might as well be hollowed out and replaced with machinery. Reprogrammed. I'm not human any more. That's what's coming through in my dreams, that's what's keeping me awake the other times. Even with my friends, the people I love, I can't seem to connect. Sometimes *they* seem like machines to me, too. Athena and Cassiopeia are like mechanical toys, just like when I was a child—I move them around this game board called romance, place them on the spaces most convenient for myself. God, what a creep! At least they're people, game pieces don't talk back, and both Athena and Cassiopeia are extremely skilled at verbal violence. Ah, I'm just babbling on. We're getting nowhere."

"Hmmm, quite the contrary. See how much you are learning about yourself. Tick off the points. Your feeling of futility about the war. Your deep hatred of the enemy, a hatred that troubles you. Your tendency toward antagonism. Your ability to hide your fears in a joking remark. Your inhuman treatment of other humans. Your inhuman feelings about yourself. No, I would say that we are getting somewhere. Now relax, let me try another approach."

Starbuck started to protest, tried to say he didn't feel satisfied by a few glib summaries about his personality, but the new fantasy began materializing around him. Again, it was a forest, but there was a softer, pastel-like quality to the colors of the trees. The dirt on the path was a lighter brown and looked sandier in texture. There were even more flowers, growing more abundantly, with more variations in their colors. He was riding again, but this time the animal beneath him was white, except for a horn on its head, a tricolored horn—white at the base, purple at the top, black in the middle—that was nearly two feet long and came to a curved point. This was not a horse, although in many respects it resembled one. Of course. It was a unicorn. He had never seen a unicorn before. Some people believed they did not exist, had never existed; others insisted they had once been plentiful on the planets Aquarus and Virgon. He had never really believed in them himself, certainly never expected to see one. Wait, he really *wasn't* seeing one. This was just as much a therapeutic fantasy as was the red knight adventure. But a much more agreeable one. He relaxed, sitting back on the unicorn's haunches, his left leg slightly pulled up onto the beautiful white animal's back. Riding into a glade, a high waterfall sliding down at a cliffside in the distance, he saw a small village along the banks of a slowmoving stream. None of the villagers, people dressed primitively in animal skins, seemed to notice him. They were all busy at tasks, some tending to gardens, others building structures, still others engaged in cleaning or landscaping. Some young people frolicked romantically in a glen outside the village. A few even younger children played games in a field. Starbuck could almost recall, from watching the patterns of their play, the names of their various games. They were not warlike games, they were the *other* kinds of play that he'd nearly forgotten about.

"I feel like joining them," he said aloud.

"Why don't you?"

"I don't know, I couldn't. I have too many duties to return to. I don't have time for useless activity."

"Useless? Is it useless to tend the soil, make a community, bring up children in a family, play freely, maintain a steady peace?"

"Well, I guess useless isn't the word. Within their own limits, or borders, I suppose a great deal of useful work is being performed. But it ignores the larger events. It's an escape really. It ignores the very real evil in the universe, evil like the Cylons and their masterplan to wipe us out."

"But the Cylons are not coming here. This is, if you will, a little backwater settlement on a little backwater planet. There is nothing here that the Cylons can use. These people can exist in peace, till their soil, enjoy their leisure, raise generations without worry of sudden ambush or despoilment by your so-called evil race of Cylons."

"I'll ignore that so-called. Anyway, I'll admit this is all very attractive. Supremely attractive. Every warrior who's ever tasted blood has dreamed of this kind of escape, someplace safe to retreat to, a haven where worries disappear."

"There are many such places on many worlds. Why don't you find one and settle down?"

Starbuck started to give the machine the book answer, the one about the weight of duty and the necessity for honor, the responsibilities toward your troubled fellow man, but he found that the words would not come easily to him. Somehow his trouble with those words was connected to these current personal problems. Duty and honor did not have much meaning for him. These days they seemed inflated from overuse. He understood what they were supposed to mean, and he had observed many of his companions give more than lip service to them, but he no longer felt a compulsion to commit to the concepts they stood for. The survivors of the destroyed twelve worlds had such a desperate need for heroes that they misused the heroic words.

"Well, I'm just not the settling kind," he finally said, reverting to the old fighter pilot cliche in order to avoid the issue. "Anyway, I'd always remember what's out beyond the village. I'd know that I'd turned coward."

"Is it cowardly to arrange your own life according to your emotional needs?"

"It is when your buddies, the buddies you left behind, are getting their vipertails shot off because you aren't there to protect them."

"Duty means more to you then."

"Not duty even. Just doing what's right."

"And that isn't duty?"

"Not always."

"I do not easily respond to cryptic utterances."

"Well, *you* join this village and stick your head in a mudhole."

"But you do admit that this life appeals to you, that you'd like, for a short while at least, to lose yourself in an idyllic setting performing useful acts of a limited nature?"

"Look, I don't even—"

Starbuck was interrupted by the low hum of the sigmawave bridge signaller that he carried in the pocket of his buckskin jacket. Its steady rhythm signified that Starbuck was ordered to the bridge on the double. Something doing.

"Well sorry, pal. Duty, acceptable or otherwise, calls. This has been fun but—"

"I will send you notice of an appointment for another session with me through the regular channels."

"Don't bother. I feel better already."

"Ah, but one session is never sufficient. We have just begun."

"You may have, but I think I've had enough."

"Nonsense. Problems like yours just don't vanish with a flippant remark from your ready tongue. Think it over. You will return to me."

"Oh, yeah? Just like your regular clientele that's keeping you so busy these days."

Starbuck fled the therapy room before the voice could produce a suitable response. As he passed through the doorway, he heard a series of small noises that sounded like mechanisms being shut off.

The corridor outside seemed even darker than before. Going along it was liking walking through the mist at the beginning of one his nightmares. He almost jumped out of his skin when a figure leaped out of the shadows and blocked his path.

"Who the hell are you?" Starbuck shouted, afraid that this individual was merely another fantasy supplied by the therapy room device, perhaps a nurse or guard whose job it was to force him back to the room. A closer view showed that the man looked to be even more of an apparition than Starbuck had first thought. He was an old man, with a dirty gray beard, wearing clothes so ancient they belonged in a museum. As he moved nearer to Starbuck, the lieutenant detected a distinct odor of ambrosa, years of it apparently, on the man's breath and mingled with the rags he wore.

"Never usually see anybody down here," the man muttered. "Most people I know are afraid to even come into these corridors."

"Who are you?"

"I'm nobody in particular. I was an engineer once, an engineer on this very ship. Before your time no doubt. And even if you were aboard during my years of duty you wouldn't have known me. Damn officers never come belowdecks, what do you care about us? I see you're a skypilot. Special person, eh?"

"Oldtimer, I have nothing against you."

"Nothing *for* me either. Bridge crew, pilots, technicians, you all leave engineers alone. How many times you spent your liberty with engineers, lieutenant?"

"Matter of fact, often. Engineers are the riskiest gamblers, and I gamble, sir. I like to play with engineers. The games become more exciting."

"Well, you're the exception then. I'll take your word for it. You look like a nice fellow, like you can handle yourself in a pinch. But what in Kobol are you doing down here, youngster? Don't you know this is the devil's pit?"

"Devil's pit? What does that mean?"

The old man's face seemed to get even older as he furrowed his brow in puzzlement. He leaned in toward Starbuck and the stale ambrosa odor became more pronounced, even muskier.

"Devil's pit. Engineers gave this place the name. See, right above us is where our fuel is stored in allegedly shatterproof containers. Could blow at any time, we all know that. Above that is the gigantic machinery that powers this glorified barge. There ain't much below this level, storage holds, little more. This is as deep as most people can go in the *Galactica*, but most people are smart and they avoid it."

"I didn't know that. I wondered, when I saw how far I had to go to get to the therapy rooms."

"Therapy rooms? What're them?"

"These rooms along this corridor."

"Don't know what you're talking about. They're the forbidden chambers. Spooky. Even I never go in 'em, and I go all over this godforsaken ship, usually without being seen. But these rooms—scared of 'em, like all the rest of the engine room crews, though I don't usually cotton to engineer superstitions. Engineers are a superstitious lot, did you know that?"

"No, I—"

"Yeah, we never really believe, no matter how much education we get, that all this here theoretical stuff really explains how things work—physics and that stuff. Lot of us greasemonkeys believe that demons activate fuel.

Ogres turn the wheels and gears. Phantoms breathe life into the engines. Silly, maybe, but that's why engineers are most often chosen priests in the many cults of the twelve worlds. I mean, we know better, but we feel comfortable with the legends and mysteries. You get it?"

"Not really."

"Maybe not. Anyway, I'd stay out of those rooms, I were you. Ghosts in them. They'll get you."

"You know, you may be right. After what I just experienced in there, I'm inclined to agree with—"

Starbuck abruptly stopped speaking as the old man, with a wicked laugh, stepped back into the shadows. Taking a very tentative step forward, he looked for the old man. However, the corridor was empty. A shudder traveled quickly through his body. Maybe there was something to the old man's talk about demons and phantoms. Maybe he was one himself. He'd heard talk about ghosts roaming the *Galactica*, former crewmen so attached to duty that they could not abandon the ship even after they had died. It was easy enough to believe such stories in these dismal deeply-shadowed hallways. He started walking quickly, prodded in part by the renewed urgency of the humming in his sigmawave bridge signaller, but even more so by his desire to get the hell out of the devil's pit.

The cockpit of his viper, for all its claustrophobic tightness, felt expansive in comparison to the therapy room's generous area and limitless fantasy vistas. And being on patrol, even a routine patrol like the present one, was infinitely preferable to contrived fantasies on horseback or astride a unicorn. It was ironic that such pretty illusions could not improve on flying a complicated construction of metal through a vivid, if presently a bit monotonous, section of space.

Back on *Galactica*'s bridge, Apollo had been somewhat curt with Starbuck, ragging him about not responding to signal fast enough. No wonder really. The captain was still reeling emotionally from the death of his wife Serina in a tragic combat with Cylons back on Kobol. Apollo's command duties had also been doubled recently because his father, Commander Adama, was in his quarters, laid up with Sagitaran flu. If all that weren't trouble enough, Apollo was struggling to be a proper normal father to his adopted son Boxey.

Poor Boxey, Starbuck thought, *that kid's problems remind me of mine when I was young. His real parents killed in a Cylon attack and all. Added to that, the loss of his foster mother not long after he'd announced so proudly that Serina and Apollo were to be his new parents. But Boxey's a tough kid, resilient like me, he'll make it.*

Apollo's orders to Starbuck to take over a routine patrol for Ensign Greenbean, who was also laid up with Sagitaran flu, were given in a clipped, tense, even testy voice. The general atmosphere on the bridge was so tense, with everyone uneasy at Apollo's persistent insistence on perfection, that it seemed another good reason to be out on patrol, away from *Galactica*.

Two further reasons for being away from the command ship were Athena and Cassiopeia. Athena had pointedly turned her back on him when he flashed his famous smile at her, snubbing him by pretending to be totally engrossed in her work at the bridge communications console. Cassiopeia, whom he'd bumped into in the corridor leading away from the bridge, congratulated him on successfully mastering the magical art of vanishing while still in front of the audience, and then she pretended that he *had* just that moment vanished and strode haughtily past him onto the bridge. Perhaps he had played them off one another once too often. Sure looked like it. On the other hand, maybe he'd paid too much attention to them. Maybe he should start looking in new directions, searching new horizons, finding new—God on Kobol, now he was beginning to think like one of those fantasy-interplay devices. He might as well throw a unicorn into one of those new horizons. Agreeable fantasies, that's all the therapies were. For all the interpretational gobbledygook, he hadn't learned a thing.

"Nothing doing out this way," said Boomer, his well-articulated speech coming clearly over the commline. "What do you think, Starbuck? Starbuck? I see your viper down there, you still in it, buddy?"

"Sorry, Boomer. Mind's just drifting off."

"Well, let's head back. This should be a sufficiently deep recon probe, enough to satisfy even Captain Apollo."

Starbuck edged his viper closer to his wingmate's craft and together they executed a precise looping turn. However, when they eased out of the loop, Starbuck's ship started drifting away from Boomer's.

"Hey, bucko, stay on course. Don't want you to get lost now."

"Sorry, I was executing mechanically. Can't seem to keep my mind on things."

"Oh great! Remind me to requisition another wingmate, case any real battle develops."

"Aw, who'd save your tail if I wasn't around?"

"About a dozen other pilots, including a couple of cadets who're gonna be giving you competition any day now, especially if you let your mind keep wandering like that."

Starbuck checked his instrument panel and realigned his viper to link up with Boomer's fast steady course.

"You know, Boomer, I think I've just come to an important decision. Like you to be the first to know."

The sound coming loud and clear over the commline was unmistakably Boomer yawning.

"I can pass on it," he said. "Your big decisions usually have all the emotional weight of a hot air balloon. And I don't choose that comparison lightly."

"You're feeling nasty today. Which is to say, your normal self."

"So okay, tell me your big decision."

"I was thinking of what my old flight instructor once said. His words just came back to me. I could almost hear him whispering over my shoulder."

"You sure you haven't got a stowaway in your cockpit?"

"No, Boomer, I'm serious. I'm tired of bantering, I want to talk straight."

Boomer, always sensitive to a buddy's mood, responded in a friendly and quite gentle voice:

"Yeah, know what you mean. I'm tired of bantering, too. Lately, case you hadn't noticed, our bantering is getting a bit tired as it is. Tell me what the ol' flight instructor said."

"Well, he used to have this big bass voice, and he said to me one day when we were both getting smashed on ambrosa and wellwater: 'Starbuck, a viper pilot only flies three vipers. The one he trains in, the one he escapes from, and the one he dies in.'"

Boomer paused a moment before commenting:

"Yeah, I see. A little pompous, but not inappropriate. Look, Starbuck, it's been a long flight, a long war. You're exhausted and it's your exhaustion that's doing most of the talking."

"Maybe. Anyway, I decided. Gambling and socializing, that's what's doing me in. In between alerts it's all gambling and socializing. I haven't even read a book in—in I don't know how long. So I'm giving up gambling and socializing. As of now."

"Look, Starbuck, in that narrow cockpit you can't even hustle a good game—and, unless you do have a pretty stowaway on board, the socializing gets pretty difficult—as of now."

"I'm *serious*, Boomer."

"So am I. And I *seriously* don't believe you. The gambling, maybe you can swear off that. A tiny maybe. But the socializing? Not a chance, Lance. Uh, uh. Not a chance."

"You wanna bet?"

Boomer laughed and seemed about to throw a smart remark back along the commline when alarm came suddenly into his voice:

"Starbuck! The scanner!"

Starbuck glanced down at his scanner and saw a thick patch of blips that unmistakably indicated Cylon raiders bearing down on them. He tensed his body and saw one of them appear near him as if by magic. The attacker was swooping down at him, highside.

"Look out, Starbuck!" Boomer shouted, just before a massive flowering of laser bursts filled the space around him. Miraculously, not a single shot hit the mark. Starbuck maneuvered his viper out of range, then whipped it around and went after his attackers. The Cylons in the raider could not react in time and Starbuck's shots hit their ship, first in the tail, then amidships, then in the nose. A brilliant flash and the Cylon ship had become miniscule pieces of space garbage.

"Starbuck! I'm in trouble!" shouted Boomer.

"You're in trouble? Well, I got appointments elsewhere but I guess I'll have to break them."

Starbuck made quick destructive work of the pair of Cylon ships that were trying to trap Boomer, but suddenly the space around him seemed crowded with Cylon spacecraft. For a moment the battle seemed to Starbuck like one of the simulation games on the *Galactica* rec level, where a series of optional kills materialized on a trio of screens and the game-player had to choose which one to dispose of in an instant or be zapped by all the attackers. Split second timing won the game. In this very real battle, Starbuck's split second timing obtained a pair of kills, but he was a shade too slow with the third marauder. As he went after it in a high-G turn, it got off a number of shots at him and suddenly his viper was rocking with the impact of a resounding lowside hit. The gauges and scanners on his control panel started throbbing, needles racking across all the numbers, flashing erratic rows of information. Red danger lights pulsed rhythmically, indicating that the main damage was in the viper's underbelly. Frantically, Starbuck's fingers hit switches and punched buttons, trying to engage systems that would bypass the ruined area. But the damage was too extensive, the bypass network could not function.

"Boomer! I'm—"

"I can see. But I got some problems of my own, old buddy. Momentarily. And here they come now. Okay fellows, line up. Oh, fine. You're fulfilling your secret fantasy of becoming sitting targets, right? There's one . . . two . . . three . . . ah, a good maneuver for a Cylon. My congratulations. The smart Cylon's the one that flees. Good-bye, red-light."

Starbuck had no time to observe any of Boomer's victories, but—knowing his wingmate's considerable flying skills intimately—he easily envisioned the lightning quick and delicately accurate maneuvers that had brought about the triple kill.

"Okay, Starbuck, pressure's off . . . for the moment. Now what's bothering your head, huh? Oh, my my. You okay?"

The concern and caution in Boomer's voice frightened Starbuck more than the impact of the hit had.

"I'll answer that after you tell me how bad it is. No little white lies, Boomer."

Boomer let out a low whistle, then said:

"Tell the truth, Starbuck, I've seen crashed vipers that looked in better shape than yours does now. The undercarriage is, well, completely gone, and you've got stuff—wires, cables, panels—sticking out a hole. All hanging out to dry, so to speak."

"None of my emergency systems are operating."

"Not surprised. It's a mystery to me how you can still transmit. Look, it's just a hop, skip, and jump to the A4477 star system, according to my scanner. We passed it on the way out. Think you can make it? I can stick by you till you find a place to land."

"Well, since my joystick feels disconnected, about all I can do is fly straight ahead."

"I'll be wetnurse. We'll get you there, bucko."

"Maybe you better head back. My old instructor used to say, 'Get going before you run out of fuel.' No sense both of us going down, with no word back to the fleet."

"Starbuck. . . ."

"Sticking with me is a bad bet."

"But you gave up gambling, remember? Anyway, I've seen you grab a pile with some of the worst bets in the history of casinos. I'll take care of myself. Always do. Okay, I've got it all licked. Straight ahead course, to **A4477**, you can reach a small delta-class planet named Antila. And you lucked out again, don't know how you do it. Stats on my charts indicate Antila's a veritable garden spot. Breathable air, tropical splendor, everything. I don't hear you thanking me."

"Wait'll I land."

It seemed only moments before the small planet came into physical view. Starbuck's eyelids were drooping. It was possible, he realized, that his air units were malfunctioning as part of the damage and that he'd blacked out a few times during the trip. He certainly felt woozy.

"Found something interesting, Starbuck. Interesting and odd."

"What is it?"

"My info about Antila. It shows there was once a human colony there, but data about it is classified. Antila was declared off limits some time ago. Survey report indicates danger but the reason for that is withheld."

"Well, Boomer, I'll let you know what I find out. Maybe there'll be another great gambling casino like the one on Carillon. You remember, where the winners were liable to become quick Ovion dinners."

"Don't remind me."

From above, Antila was an impressive sight, its land

areas looking something like a patchwork quilt in pastel colors.

"Okay Boomer, take off. Report back."

"Not until I know you're down."

"Down? Where else I got to go? If I don't make it, I promise you'll be the first to know."

"I'll be back with a clean uniform and some get well quick cards before you know it."

"On the uniform—make sure it's the one with the blue piping. You know, just in case I meet a lady."

"Thought you gave up socializing along with gambling. . . ."

Boomer started to laugh, then stopped abruptly.

"What'm I laughing about? With your luck, you're probably going to fall into a harem down there. Second thought, I think my best shot is to come down with you. I'm tired of being the messenger, while you drop into the good life and—"

"Boomer!"

"Okay, okay. I'm going."

"Be seeing you. I hope."

"No doubt about it."

Starbuck did not even look up to see Boomer peel off and head into the distance. He was getting woozier. The ship seemed to bounce roughly as it passed into Antila's atmosphere. With half its systems out of whack, it was lucky for Starbuck that his viper didn't simply burn out when it encountered atmosphere. He tried the joystick again. It slid around aimlessly in its square slot. He found if he pressed it forward he could make the nose of his ship dip slightly, a maneuver he performed as he slipped by a thin cloud layer. Below him the patchwork quilt seemed to fade a bit and change into greenery, water, jungle. Looked like he was headed for the jungle part. He pulled the joystick back, hoping against hope that he could level the viper off and choose his own landing spot. There was no response from it. If he pulled at it, he felt it would slide upwards right out of its slot. The nose of the ship seemed pointed downwards, at too precarious an angle. This wasn't going to be a crash landing, it'd be a full-fledged crash. *Good thing Boomer's not here to see me buy the agricultural complex*, Starbuck thought, *goodbye old buddy, good—*

Starbuck blacked out just as his ship seemed to reach the luminescently green tops of the trees in this bizarre Antilean jungle forest.

CHAPTER TWO

For the third time this work period, Spectre's chief aide broke down. First its red light slid to a gradual stop and blinked out. Then its arms and legs stopped functioning, leaving it in a grotesque pose that might have been amusing had it not been so inconvenient and irritating. One of its arms pointed forward, the other flung back; one leg was raised to take a step, the other was flat to the ground. Spectre watched it teeter for a moment, then slowly, agonizingly fall forward, landing on the ground with a loud thump and a series of small pings. Spectre had a momentary urge to kick the out-of-commission centurion in the chest with his heavy metal foot, but then he might do something damaging to his own circuits. The warriors of his garrison would be working correctly if it were not for the excruciating humidity of Antila. Spectre did not mind that his aide had malfunctioned, malfunctioning was a fact of life here, but the series of small pings annoyed him greatly. They meant that this Cylon construct would have to go into the shop to be worked on. It would probably be out of service for at least another work period. Spectre's garrison was already understaffed. Almost half his warriors were down, all at various stages of being fixed in the shop. Most of the repair technicians, whom Spectre had taken care to keep in a controlled-atmosphere environment, were fortunately in good working order, although occasionally subject to leaks from the outside air.

Spectre beeped his thumb and a nearby pair of centurions came running.

"Torso malfunction, I believe," he said to the medical

29

team. "Take him to a pulmonary circuit specialist."

Obeying instantly, the centurion medical team lifted the body of their fallen comrade and, at a lumbering walk, carried him away. Raising and beeping his thumb again, Spectre signalled for another aide, and one joined him quickly.

"Your name?" Spectre asked the new arrival.

He usually forgot the names he had given his creations. How could he remember? They were all assemblages of machinery decked out in identical Cylon uniforms. He had tried name tags for a while, but the printing tended to be quickly obscured by mudstains and rust. This planet was against him, clearly. Days of rain, continual mud; muddy, rusting warriors; an army of muddy children making their loathsome sneak attacks on the fuel dumps and artillery depots. Those children— they'd even taken to ambushing patrols. Spectre had to cut down on the number of patrols, since he could not afford to lose personnel that way. The children dragged their victims into the bushes and undergrowth, threw them into the murky waters of the swamps, sometimes even dismantled them—all of which made repairs impossible and further depleted Spectre's depopulated garrison.

The new aide announced that his name was Hilltop. Spectre did not even recall naming this one. Obviously, when he had completed the circuit that animated it, he must have glanced out a window and caught sight of the top of a hill. Spectre tended to name his creations by that sort of method—a bit pedestrian but easier than thinking about it, and certainly preferable to preserving the appellation of the actual Cylon who had once inhabited the Centurion outfit, before dying of one of the numerous diseases that the Cylons had been so susceptible to on Antila. In order to maintain his garrison at minimum acceptable strength, Spectre had had to build his own robot versions of Cylons—and good jobs they were, too, except for their tendency to break down at odd times. He could have requested higher commands to assign more warriors, but he did not want the Cylons to know of his rebuilding efforts and, anyway, replacements would just have succumbed to the dangerous Antila climate. Besides, the loss of combat personnel was generally viewed as a significant weakness in command and could become the kind of detail included in a report that would seriously affect promotion. Spectre, true bureaucrat that he was, wanted no bad marks in his personnel file. So, it had been preferable to stick with his own creations. The machines were more efficient than their sentient originals, anyway. Spectre, one of the most versatile ambulatory cybernetic sentiences ever manufactured, had always believed in the superiority of his kind.

"What is my duty, Commander Spectre, sir?" Hilltop asked in the polite, if a bit scratchy, voice that Spectre had programmed for ultimate courtesy. Courtesy was important to Spectre, and he enjoyed the sound of it.

"You are to supervise the shifting of the main fuel dump closer to headquarters. The children's attacks have come too near to it lately, our recent losses in personnel make it impossible to guard effectively. We can't afford to lose valuable fuel."

Actually, they *could* afford to lose a significant amount of fuel. Spectre was a hoarder by nature. During his tenure on Antila, he had managed—through adroit manipulations of supply forms and clever insights into the habits of supply officers everywhere—to stockpile materials of all kinds, shapes, and forms. He had rooms filled to the ceiling with items he had acquired. Some materials were not even useful at the present time, but Spectre believed in storing away for the future and covering all contingencies. Still, the fuel, by his standards, had become something of a problem, even though he had requisitioned enough of it to power a larger headquarters than his, plus a fleet quadruple the size of the few outdated flying vehicles he had managed to obtain.

The Cylon Spacecraft Bureau was decidedly difficult to hoodwink, and further was notoriously stingy in its allocations. Spectre had yet to find a way around their latest set of restrictions. He would eventually, he was sure. He was superb at finding ways to get what he wanted without offending officers above him. He understood bureaucracy so well, and his data banks were so replete with bureaucratic information, that he could discover a route to any type of supply so long as he had an urgent need for it and such a route existed. Spectre had been designed to be the perfect bureaucrat and, when the dampness of Antila was not damaging his circuits or creating a bypass where none was supposed to be, he *was* the perfect bureaucrat.

He adjusted his anti-rust shield as he left his office and walked into the morning mist that lay like a shroud across this swampy area of Antila landscape. It was important that he stay operative—a healthy leader was an efficient leader. Long ago, when he had been only an advisor to an actual Cylon commander, his boss had been meticulous in seeing to the care and protection of Spectre. After that commander had succumbed to a particularly ugly plague, a sickness that so affected his brain (or, in his case, brains), that he removed a real Cylon from the chain of command and installed Spectre in his place. Spectre became an executive officer, a position he held only a short time, since the officers ahead of him died of several interesting and various Antila diseases. Antila was an unattractive backwater planet and a low-priority assignment, Spectre knew, but where else could he have risen legally and officially to command of a garrison? Even though he hated the place, he hesitated to put in for a transfer. Real Cylons might bust him back to a lesser rank, and he liked being commander, liked it very much.

A pair of centurions detached themselves from the fuel dump work detail to report to Spectre and Hilltop.

Behind them, other warriors of the garrison were busily and mechanically moving fuel drums and gear from their former unprotected location to a place inside the garrison walls.

"Your work is satisfactory," Spectre told the centurions after they had formally made their report. The red lights on their helmets brightened momentarily, a signal of satisfaction which Spectre had programmed into his creations. Since one could never know a real Cylon's opinions from observation, Spectre had installed this improvement on his own creations.

"Hilltop!" Spectre called.

"Yes, Commander sir."

"After the fuel and materials are safely inside the fortress walls, fortify the walls. Fill in cracks, increase guard posts, set traps—you know the drill."

"Yes, I do, but Commander sir—"

"Yes, Hilltop?"

"Won't it be dangerous for the garrison buildings to have so much volatile fuel so close to them?"

"Not at all. The containers are triple thick with impenetrable metals. Spontaneous explosions within are extremely rare and usually minimized by container thickness. We must protect our supplies from our enemy, especially since their raids have increased. Go to it, Hilltop."

"Yes, Commander sir. By your command."

Spectre watched the centurions labor for some time. Their work was admirable, timed precisely and with a meticulous teamwork that sentient beings were capable of only rarely. That was why he preferred his recycled Cylons to the genuine article.

"Commander sir," interrupted another centurion.

"Yes, uh—um, your name, soldier?"

"Treebark, sir."

"What is your business, Treebark?"

"Guard patrol craft in the middle trisector intercepted

two vipercraft piloted by humans, sir. Communications Center officer would appreciate your presence for his report."

"Yes, at once."

The centurion gave the complicated four-stage salute that Spectre had invented to replace the overly-brusque, stiffly ceremonial regular Cylon salute. Treebark accompanied his leader through the garrison gate and to the communications center. The news that there were colonial vipers in the area pleased Spectre. There were scant military reasons for his garrison's existence, after all, and this news would fortify any report he made, enabling him to justify the garrison's continued presence on this bleak planet.

Inside communications center, the news did not please him quite so much. Six of the seven raiders on patrol had been obliterated by the pair of vipers, much too great a loss of personnel. He would have to alter the casualty numbers on any dispatch pertaining to the incident. Better yet, he would not mention the loss of personnel or vehicles.

However, the results of the battle had more dire ramifications. This patrol represented the last set of Spectre's Cylon constructs that were programmed to pilot. The lone survivor of the patrol could not defend the planet alone, and the garrison had already sustained too many losses to detach any more warriors for piloting duties. They would have to get along without pilots for a while, until he could figure out how to manufacture a few— perhaps he could work out something in a new design from his stockpile of materials. For the moment, the best he could do was listen to the report of his communications officer.

"One viper escaped, sir, and it is presumably returning to origination point. The second was crippled by a hit on its underside and was last observed heading toward Antila. We are tracking the craft."

"Order the patrol to return."

Spectre wondered, as the communications officer turned to his console to follow the order, whether such a primitive construct could appreciate the irony in calling a single surviving raider a full patrol. After the officer had transmitted the order, Spectre commanded:

"Contact the base star."

He did not particularly want to communicate with the base star at this time, but official procedure said he should. Right now he should do his best to impress the superior officers with his efficiency and military prowess. That might mean embellishing the data just a trifle. Spectre did not mind that. His career had progressed so smoothly precisely because of his abilities to embellish information.

He was also pleased that the base star, commanded by the renegade human Baltar, was too far away to intervene at this time. Baltar's second-in-command could pose something of a problem. He was an ambulatory computer named Lucifer, a construct of a later series than Spectre's—and Lucifer never missed a chance to remind his presumed inferior of the difference in their respective classes.

Still, as long as he kept them at a distance, Spectre could handle them. By keeping ahead of whomever he had to deal with, Spectre could handle anybody.

Lucifer had been congratulating himself on how well everything was going. The ship was in perfect running condition, and operating efficiently at all levels of procedure. Baltar, the nominal commander of the base star, was staying out of Lucifer's way and not making those blunders that humans were so prone to. The area of space they were patrolling was quite peaceful. True, they had lost track of the *Galactica* since its escape from Kobol, but *Galactica* was Baltar's obsession—Baltar's and that of the supreme commander, Imperious Leader. Lucifer was not obsessed with the humans' sole surviving battlestar and did not care if they ever located it again. He did not want to have to concern himself with *Galactica*'s extremely resourceful crew again. Although he did have some fond memories of one of them, a brash young lieutenant they had held prisoner on the base ship for a short time. What was the man's name? Starshine? Starluck? Something like that.

Aside from the minor annoyances, matters seemed so much in order that Lucifer considered turning himself off for a while and letting subordinates take over. There appeared to be nothing to disturb the even flow of events aboard ship, and Lucifer felt content. If he had been human, he might have worried, since most humans know that such contentment is dangerous, that just when you feel everything is going well, that's the time when something is about to go wrong.

Something went wrong.

Its name was Spectre.

As soon as Lucifer saw the familiar visage on his screen, and recalled what a scheming, deceptive, ambitious representative of their species Spectre was, Lucifer knew—without even a review of his data banks—that he was in trouble. His first inclination was to break abruptly the communication and pretend that it had not happened. However, he was programmed for a meticulous attention to duty (a program he had designed for himself, after all), so he had to listen to Spectre's report.

If the sudden reappearance of Spectre in Lucifer's existence were not enough, Baltar now swaggered into the command sphere while Spectre was beginning to give his report. The news roused the human out of his lethargy and an approximation of life began to appear in his beady eyes.

"Who, uh, who is that, Lucifer?" Baltar asked.

"Antila garrison commander reporting."

"Antila."

Lucifer ritualistically explained that Antila was an obscure outpost in Omega Sector. *Obscure*? he thought— *if Spectre had not chosen to make this communication the outpost would have been completely forgotten.*

"Its commander's name is Spectre . . . I believe. Like me he is an ambulatory cybernetic development, but from another series. Before my time. Rather limited in ability, actually."

"Limited, eh? He's a *commander*, is he not? Even of an out-of-the-way outpost, that is some achievement for one of you thinking *machines*."

Baltar had a way of emphasizing the word *machine* when he talked to Lucifer, especially when he did so to remind him that not only was he a subordinate on this ship, he was subordinate to a human and not a Cylon! Lucifer did not enjoy the implications of the word machine as Baltar used it. Baltar meant that Lucifer was merely an arrangement of metal without any genuine sentience. Apparently the man had forgotten that Lucifer had told him that he had a soul, one that he had created himself and housed in his right shoulder. Lucifer felt that the biggest miscalculation he had ever made was saving Baltar, already a traitor to his own race, from a deserved execution by the Cylons and then grooming him for an advisory role. He had not suspected that Baltar would exploit his abilities to grab away the base-star command that Lucifer should have had. Well, all that was now oil flushed out a chute, and Lucifer had to go on, doing the best he could, which meant finding ways to circumvent the often foolish plans that Baltar conceived.

Baltar gestured Lucifer out of his seat and replaced him at the console, his narrow eyes narrowed further in a squint at the visage of Spectre on the screen in front of him.

"Spectre, I am commander here. I wish to hear your report."

Although an ambulatory cybernetic sentience could not duplicate a human or Cylon facial expression, Lucifer noticed that Spectre tilted his head slightly, raised his left shoulder, and leaned toward the recording camera, a trio of movements that gave the illusion of an expression of sincere concern. Lucifer now remembered just why the sudden appearance of Spectre had disturbed him. He could not trust Spectre.

"Honored Baltar, sir, I recognize the privilege of reporting to you directly. You honor myself and my series."

"Fine. Just fine. Report, Spectre."

The tone of Spectre's voice became more obviously regulated. The limb that was out of sight had probably made an adjustment in vocality in order to present the illusion of conversational intimacy. Lucifer never stooped to such mechanical tricks. How sly this Spectre was!

"Sir, we have intercepted two viper fighters and captured one."

Baltar glanced up at Lucifer, a supercilious pleased smile on his repellently human face.

"Excellent, Spectre, really excellent. And the pilot of the captured craft, have you interrogated him?"

"Ah . . . the patrol that apprehended him has not yet returned."

Why, Lucifer wondered, was he so sure that Spectre was lying? Was he so prejudiced against a different, albeit inferior, class of ambulatory computer that he could not judge it fairly?

"Are you aware of the general order concerning captured human pilots, Spectre?" Baltar asked.

"Oh yes, sir. I read and record every general order and memorandum that is sent out from base star headquarters. You wish me to discover, through intense interrogation, even including the risking of the prisoner's life, the present position of the Battlestar *Galactica*."

"You understand the order perfectly, Spectre."

"Naturally."

Spectre's attitude of self-confidence drew an even broader grin from Baltar. His eyes seemed to say about Spectre, this is *my* kind of officer. If Lucifer had been human, he would have cringed at that moment.

"I shall await your next communication," Baltar said. "And Spectre?"

"Yes, sir?"

"You have a wonderful opportunity here. Use it well."

"Oh, I will, sir. You can depend on me."

"I do believe I can, Spectre, I do believe I can. I will be waiting. . . ."

"By your command."

Spectre's image faded gently from the screen. Another effect controlled by Spectre, Lucifer thought. Baltar stood up, wearing his arrogance like a cloak around him. His tiny eyes blinked a couple of times, and he raised his left eyebrow as he said:

"Well, Lucifer, this Spectre does seem to have done rather well . . . for an early model."

Baltar started to laugh, obviously enjoying his dig at his second in command.

"Early models have their uses," Lucifer said sullenly, while considering half a dozen uses he had in mind for Spectre.

Spectre turned away from the communications console to find Hilltop now standing at his side.

"You were listening?" Spectre asked his new aide.

"Yes, Commander sir. You did inform them that we had captured the pilot when in fact we don't know where he—"

"I know, I know. That is called command privilege, Hilltop. Learn it well. We shall require a search party—"

"I have already dispatched a search party, sir."

"Very good. You do learn well."

"What if the pilot evades the searchers?"

"Impossible."

Although Spectre was aware that of course the pilot could evade his warriors, he had also calculated that, since the human was not familiar with the terrain and was quite possibly injured, the odds were on Spectre's side. Like the true bureaucrat he was, he had learned that a confident attitude and demeanor could cover up an array of minor errors of detail. In fact, Spectre believed that he had postulated all the possibilities already and had devised an explanation, diversion, or prevarication to cover any eventuality.

CHAPTER THREE

FROM MIRI'S BOOK:
Another unicorn dead. One of the wild ones. I think it had been attacked, perhaps by a lion, although there were no wounds or marks of battle on the parts of it I could see. It looked peaceful really. Its head was lying at the base of a tree along the bank of a stream. Its horn had hooked onto a gnarled, snakelike root, and its body, prevented from sliding any further, was only half in the muddy water. I knew if I cut off its horn, the heavy animal would slide all the way in. But I needed the horn. I'm almost out of medicines. It is sad that such a beautiful animal has to die in order for me to make a curing potion. I cut through the horn. As always, my knife slid easily through it. Instinctively I made a grab at its head as it started to slip away from me. It went beneath the water so gently that I wasn't able to see any ripples through the thin mist which clings to the water.

I heard sounds on the other side of the stream, the unmistakable squeaky sounds of a bunch of the tincans stumbling through underbrush, on patrol no doubt. I decided to spy on them, see what kind of strange event could remove the tincans from the security of their fortress. They so rarely leave it nowadays. They don't even come out to trap us any more.

When the sounds of the patrol had somewhat receded in the distance, I placed the unicorn's horn in my pack, found a free vine and swung across the stream. I thought

41

I saw, in dim outline, the shape of the dead unicorn resting peacefully just beneath the surface of the water.

Earlier I had heard sounds in the sky, but the morning mist had been too heavy for me to see anything. The sounds were definitely mechanical, suggesting a flying vehicle of some sort. Kyle says they are spacecraft and can fly across vast reaches of space, like the spaceship that brought us here. Kyle tells a lot of stories. I don't always know which ones are true. Kyle is younger than I, after all. Children like tales.

The sounds in the sky ended with a strange high whistle and the rustle of something heavy falling through trees far away. I thought I felt the ground vibrate slightly beneath me when the sounds ended in a muffled thud. Normally I'd have investigated, but I had more important business to attend to—tracking the path of the fleeing unicorn.

I stayed right behind the patrol for a short distance, noting that they were heading toward the area from which the sounds of the falling vehicle had come. Sometimes I was right behind the rearmost guard and could have touched him, given him a nudge that would have undoubtedly pushed him over, but I didn't want the patrol to know I was there. After a while, they took a wrong turn, one definitely away from the area of the earlier sounds. Tincans are poor at tracking. I decided to see if I could locate whatever it was that had fallen from the skies before they did.

It was not too hard to find.

The wreckage was on a spit of sand surrounded by reeds, in the middle of a swampy area. Metal, in hunks, pieces, and jagged shards, lay about. The main craft, what was left of it, sat at an angle and it looked like a touch could unbalance it and send it plunging into the water.

I was about to investigate, when there was a movement in the upper part of the wreckage. A transparent canopy atop the ship shifted a bit, then slowly rose into the air. Framed by the mist, the movement spooked me and I scrunched down where I was, in a clump of bush. A head seemed to emerge out of the wreckage and for a moment I thought it was floating alone, bodiless. But that was an optical trick. The head was actually connected to a body. Laboriously, the man pulled himself out of his ship.

He was a tall man, slim but with a definite hint of solid muscle. His hair was as long as Kyle's, but blonde. His face, well, I thought he looked like a god. I had not seen a man that attractive in some time, a good long time. After all, except for my clandestine visits to the prison, I never see an adult. All my time is spent with children much younger than I. For whatever reason, libidinous or otherwise, I liked this young pilot immediately, even though he was in a dazed and nearly unconscious state.

He virtually tumbled out of the opening in his ship and into swamp water. I thought of the unicorn sliding so gently beneath the water's surface, but this time I was ready to spring forward and save the man before his head went under. Fortunately he recovered a bit and propped himself up against the side of his vehicle, his spaceship as Kyle might call it. With his right hand he felt his leg and winced. Even from my distant vantage point, I could see that the leg was bleeding, possibly broken. He looked around, eyes bleary. He was clearly trying to get his bearings, trying to figure out what he was doing in this dismal misty swamp.

I was about to reveal myself to him and offer help, when I heard the sound of the tincans' patrol, clanking through the forest behind me. The man obviously heard the same sound, for his head lifted and, his eyes now clearer and somewhat frightened, he leaned a bit toward the sound. Before I could call to him, he pulled himself around his ship, moving very quickly for a man who had to drag a hurt leg behind him. I wanted to call out to him, but couldn't. The patrol might detect my position, although tincans weren't usually adept at finding anything. The safer course for me was to remain concealed and quiet.

I could hear the man splashing through the water, then some muffled noises on the opposite bank. The patrol was getting closer. I definitely could not call out to him. Nor could I swim across the water without leading the patrol right to the pilot. Instead, I had to watch the pilot disappear into the mist. No matter, I knew. I could locate him again later. For the moment I held position.

The patrol appeared, not far from my original hiding place. A tincan arm pointed toward the wreckage and a different tincan head nodded in agreement. They took a package from a shoulder pack, an inflatable boat, and rode across the narrow passage to the wreckage. It was clear that they were deliberately keeping their arms high from the water's surface. Tincans are afraid of rust, Kyle says, that's why, if they go near the water at all, they act so oddly.

I watched them inspect the wreckage. One of them climbed through the hole from which the pilot had emerged. Another took a communicating device out of a compartment in his arm and spoke into it. I couldn't hear what he said, but obviously he was reporting that the pilot escaped. A third tincan noticed some trampled-down reeds and pointed toward the bank. Quite accurately, actually. It was almost exactly where the man had pulled himself out of the water.

I realized I could help the man not one bit by crouching and watching the enemy track him down and corner him. My best move was to find Kyle and the rest of his band.

As soon as I was far enough away from the patrol, I started running. Kyle would be in the cave, I knew, and it was there that I found him, looking as petulant and surly as ever.

CHAPTER FOUR

Starbuck awoke to find the underside of a leaf dangling in his face. At first he could not focus upon it, nor could he figure out what he was doing staring up at a leaf. Gradually, feeling the wet ground beneath him and seeing the high curved tree roots around him, he realized that somehow he had fallen asleep in a hollow at the base of a tree. His head rested against a thick lumpy patch of moss on the tree's trunk. He felt something like he had felt years ago when he used to curl up in a big armchair back home, an ancient piece of furniture that had been his foster father's favorite. Gawr had won it in a raffle and, even though it was far too lumpy and was covered by a grainy hard-textured upholstery, he had convinced himself that it was the best chair in the universe. Starbuck was not sure whether or not he was pleased. Actually the chair had never been too comfortable and the hard lumpy ground and the uneven surface of the moss was a trifle too much like the original.

Slowly the leaf, drooping down at him from a low-hanging branch, came into focus. He was fascinated by the leaf's bluish green color and its almost perfect triangular shape with rounded corners. He reached up and touched it. Its surface was furry, with miniature thorns all over it. The thorns, little spikes really, were not sharp enough to puncture his skin, but they did create a mildly painful tingling sensation in his fingertips. Touching the other side of the leaf gently, he pulled it closer to him. The branch did not give easily, but he was able to move it enough to bring the leaf into a better light. He saw that it was really more blue than green, and that there

was a speckled effect caused by a deeper shade of blue
at the tips of the tiny thorns. The veins of the leaf were
unusually thick, almost as thick as human veins. He
wondered if a liquid would spurt out if he punctured one
of its veins with his thumbnail, and if the liquid would
be something he could drink. On this strange planet he
could imagine becoming a vampire of leaves, a vege-
tarian vampire. He decided it was best not to puncture
the vein or to mar the leaf any further. He let it go,
watched the branch vibrate a couple of times upon re-
lease, then come to quick almost rigid motionlessness.

What, he wondered suddenly, was he doing taking
up nature study now, with a platoon of Cylons scouring
the forest for him? As the memory of his flight from the
Cylons came back to him, he realized that he had been
listening for some time to clanking and rustling sounds—
evidently Cylons making havoc of greenery. It sounded
like the search party was coming near.

He tried to scrunch down further into the hollow. But
that, he perceived immediately, was not going to work.
If they came anywhere near the tree, there was a good
chance they would see him. The roots were not high
enough, the single overhanging branch not enough
cover.

Trying to pull himself up, he felt again the throbbing
pain in his leg. Each throb felt like a fist inside his leg
ramming at the same already hemorrhaging area over
and over. Grabbing at the drooping branch, he found it
to be remarkably firm and unresilient. Using it as lever,
he stood up. The effort exhausted him, however, and he
could not move for a moment. Looking outward, at the
bizarrely beautiful and complex network of jungle, he
realized suddenly that the gray and black color at the
center of his view was not vegetation at all, but a Cylon
warrior looking right at him. His heart started beating
faster and it was all he could do to remain motionless.
The Cylon did not seem to be seeing him, even though
he was looking right at him. There was something wrong,

what was it? It was like a missing piece in one of those
Tauron holographic puzzles—you could tell a chunk of
it was missing but the three dimensionality of the images
obscured the location of the vacant area. Then he perceived what was wrong with the picture in front of him.
The red light. There was no red light. Or, rather, there
was a red light but it was not functioning, not moving
from side to side on the Cylon helmet as it normally
would do. This Cylon warrior was not moving at all. It
had reached this part of the forest, right next to Starbuck's tree, and died standing up.

In spite of the pain in his leg and the proximity of the
patrol, Starbuck's easily aroused curiosity was piqued.
He *had* to go and inspect this stalled Cylon. Carefully
raising his hurt leg over the lowest root with his hands
and taking care to place it gently on the ground on the
other side, he managed to take a step away from the
tree. The ground between him and the Cylon was fairly
level, just a few mysterious small fanguslike plants that
flattened like a sponge under his feet, and he found he
could limp to the Cylon without appreciable difficulty.

He came at the Cylon from the left side, cautious
because he might, after all, be mistaken—this apparently
lifeless being could actually be using some devious new
combat trick, luring the enemy by pretense of complete
inertia. When he stood next to it, he reached out and
touched the Cylon on the shoulder.

"Hi, big boy, wanna dance?" he whispered.

Clearly this was not a dancing Cylon. Starbuck's
nudge did, however, cause it to move. It rocked forward
and backward, nearly fell over, then righted itself.
Touching the warrior more gently a second time, Starbuck traced a path from its helmet, checking the unmoving red light, down its metallic tunic to its ammo
belt. The surface was smooth and cold everywhere.

Starbuck wondered what, in the interests of science,
he should do. This was, after all, the first Cylon that
anybody had encountered that had died a *natural* death.

There were scientists on the *Galactica* who would donate the key to their medicine cabinet to have a shot at examining a naturally dead specimen. This moment could be historic, even. What kept Starbuck's name out of the history books, however, was that he did not have a single notion of how to take advantage of the opportunity.

Well, he had to try. He reached an arm around the figure and found that he could lift it easily. Were it not for his hurt leg, he could have carried the damn thing on his shoulders. Now, that made no sense. A Cylon killed on the battlefield could only be lifted by two or three humans. How could this one be so light? It felt as if there were nothing inside its uniform. He remembered the red knight of his therapy room fantasy. This Cylon's lightness reminded him of a suit of armor without a knight in it. Could it be that this was not a dead Cylon at all, but merely an abandoned uniform?

Setting the warrior, or warrior-shell, down, he continued his investigation. At the lower center of the torso he found a small thin box, welded to the body. He'd never seen anything like that on any dead Cylon. He pried at it, but the sealing was too firm. Whatever this creature was, it was lighter than a real Cylon and if, as Starbuck suspected, the box contained a cybernetic programming device, it was apparently powered electronically.

The clanking sound of the search party trudging through some nearby foliage interrupted Starbuck's research. As he started to move away, looking for a suitable hiding place, he became acutely conscious of the leg pain. It was getting worse, as if whatever was affected was growing or spreading. Struggling over a fallen tree, he caught his bad leg in a branch and fell forward, his face sliding into a tangled growth of blue and purple flowers. These were not the kind of blooms you took to a loved one or sick friend; their odor was noxious, and he almost choked on it. The effort of disentangling his leg from the branch made his leg hurt more and he nearly lost consciousness. Wincing, he painfully and slowly slid his leg off the trunk of the tree. But now he could not stand up again, and the Cylon patrol seemed to be getting closer. He could not care. The pain would kill him first and, besides, he was giving in to the need to be unconscious. Blissfully unconscious.

He slid easily into a dream. His foster mother Doreen was chatting with Cassiopeia, who was nodding her pretty blonde haired head vigorously and often. Starbuck crawled closer to them (they were seated on the edge of his childhood bed, the one decorated with the decals of early-series vipers). When he got in range of their voices, he heard Doreen advising Cassie about the kind of foods he liked and how to prepare them. That's not fair, he said to them, it's a conspiracy. I'm not the marrying type. And I'm giving up socializing along with gambling. But they paid him no attention, he was invisible to them.

Abruptly they changed, Doreen became Gawr and Cassiopeia became Athena. Gawr told Athena she was wasting her time with Starbuck. Even if he chose her, life with Starbuck would be dreadful because he had no conception of real love. Love for him was a kind of fantasy game where you rode unicorns and pretended to be a hero. Starbuck could not communicate with Gawr and Athena either. A moment later they, too, had disappeared. In their place was a white unicorn, looking something like the one in his therapy room fantasy. It was prancing nervously but slowly toward him. He was no longer in a jungle. Now he lay in a pleasant green meadow. The unicorn's head leaned down toward him and sniffed at him.

"Don't worry," Starbuck said to it, "I'll make a first class dinner. Colonial warrior, medium rare."

He fully expected the unicorn to talk back, since this was a dream. The animal only continued to stare and sniff. Joining it was a mottled gray and white unicorn. It touched Starbuck's shoulder briefly with its horn. Star-

buck sat up with a start and shook his head unbelievingly.
He could have sworn the unicorn had spoken. Reaching
up he grasped the unicorn's horn with one hand and
concentrated. Well-being was communicated, and friendly
concern. Suddenly he knew he would be all right.

"Sure," he said, "everything's all right. In *dreams*."

"You're not dreaming."

At first he thought that the gray-white unicorn had
spoken again, but looking up he saw a young man sitting
on the white unicorn. This youngster had obviously been
the speaker. He was dressed in a green tunic over dark
brown trousers. There was a flat green cap on his head,
under whose brim flowed fairly long brown hair. He
looked no more than fourteen or fifteen years old.

"You'll be all right," said the other rider, a strikingly
attractive young woman, who resembled the young man
and wore similar garments. She seemed, however, to be
older than the boy, and a little taller. She was slim, but
hardly boyish, and had long dark brown hair, just a shade
darker than the boy's. Her hair reached almost to her
waist. She was lovely, just right for a pleasant dream
of a pleasant meadow. But wait, both said this wasn't
a dream. They were right, it wasn't. Gawr advising
Athena to drop Starbuck had been a dream, but he had
awakened from it. To see unicorns? That made even less
sense.

He would have worried about it further, but the pain
in his leg interfered. He moaned, winced, closed his
eyes, and was immediately asleep again.

CHAPTER FIVE

FROM MIRI'S BOOK:
We had a close call rescuing the pilot. Kyle, who hadn't wanted to come back for the man in the first place, continued to be sullen all the way to the clearing where we finally located our quarry. The man was startled awake, but looked at us as if we were just another episode in a dream he was having, and quickly went back to sleep.

"Guess I'll have to heft him up onto Demon," Kyle muttered, his voice sarcastic and angry.

He had a tough time lifting the man, who outweighed him a good bit, onto the back of Demon. The task would have been easier if I had helped him. But he has to ask me for help, he knows that. I won't help him unless he asks. He didn't ask.

Once the man lay limp across Demon's gleaming white back, Kyle swung up behind him and said:

"Let's ride, sister."

He's taken to calling me sister. It provides him some sort of childish amusement. Anytime he says something with the word sister in it, he's able to deepen his voice till it sounds grownup. Most of the time his voice breaks when he gets emotional, and he's always getting emotional about *something*.

We had hardly turned around to head back for the cave, when a tincan voice, that obnoxious noise which reminds me of a metallic gargle, ordered us to halt. Kyle leaned forward, his hands gripping Demon's mane tightly, and was about to make a run for it. Typical of him, ready to act before thinking, before assessing the situation. The tincans surrounded us, their monstrous bulky rifles pointed at us. We might have been able to escape on our own, but I thought it was a fool's run. The only thing that made it possible was Kyle's tendency to act the fool when he could put action into a heroic light.

One of the tincans said to the apparent leader:

"Our commander will be pleased with us. Not only do we capture the human who is our objective, but we also trap the two biggest pests among the children."

"Yes, Mudhole," the leader said. "This will definitely bring us praise from Spectre."

It's hard to discern anything particularly meaningful in the tone, pitch, or rhythm of a tincan voice, but I was sure I heard a distinct squeak of self-satisfaction from this one.

The patrol, marching in clumsy uncoordinated step, started to close the circle around us.

I looked at Kyle.

He looked back at me.

I nodded.

It was time to call in the troops.

Kyle lifted his horn quickly to his mouth and blew a long steady blast. The tincans, who should have known by now what the sound signified, merely kept advancing. Behind them the children of Kyle's band started dropping from trees, squirming out from under bushes, running into a clearing from hiding places where they'd been silently watching and waiting for the signal. I caught a glimpse of my sister Ariadne, swinging a branch almost twice her size—she's twelve and small for her age—with which she felled a tincan by ramming it against the back of its legs. I saw my twin brothers Nilz and Robus, ganging up on the tincan leader together, one aiming at the upper part of the body, the other at the lower. Another tincan clanked to the ground. I saw Laughing Jake and Chubby Marta and Ratzi and Herbert the Singer and Melysa and Jergin and the Genie; I saw members of our band whose names I could not immediately recall; I saw twenty-seven children, ranging in age from six to thirteen, all of them assaulting the tincan patrol, each with a clear objective and all working deftly and with despatch. As soon as all the tincans were grounded—they have great difficulty in righting themselves with any speed—Kyle blew a short blast on the horn and we cleared out. Kyle and I on our mounts, the children vanishing quickly back into the forest.

From a prone position, a couple tincans managed a couple shots, but the beams went well over our heads.

Touching the back of Rogue's head, I urged him to go faster. Picking up the thought, his head bobbed up and down slightly, and we raced forward. Past Kyle on Demon. Kyle had the man as extra weight and, besides, has no telepathic link with Demon, a steed who would reject any of his orders anyway.

We took the man to the cave instead of base camp. Although the tincans had not discovered the present camp, it was too open and didn't afford the proper situation for the curing of the pilot. The tincans would never find the cave simply because they would have to pass through water to get to it. Tincans avoid water.

As we rode along I could sense some of the advance guard of Kyle's band, using vines to swing from tree to tree, their movement a barely detectable rustle all around us. Three horn blasts in the distance—Herbert the Singer letting us know that we were not being followed. We took the most direct route to the cave, crossing the lake by the curving pathway of rocks we had carefully placed in it, then we rode up the hillside, and through the middle waterfall. Once in a while, the man stirred and looked around, but, dazed by his pain and confused by the landscape, he quickly lost consciousness again. I was eager to get him inside the cave and onto a straw palette where I could take care of him properly. From his wasted pallor, I didn't have much time before he would be

beyond the point where my salves and potions would
work.

Ratzi had reached the cave ahead of us and set a
cookpot on the fire. The tantalizing odors of vegetable
stew came to us as we entered the cave's main chamber.
I realized how hungry I'd become. But, before eating,
I had to attend to my new patient.

Ratzi helped Kyle take the man off Demon's back.
Kyle, as usual, didn't even speak to her. Ratzi, who is
two years younger than Kyle and quite in love with him,
will do anything he asks. She is usually mooneyed and
always redcheeked. Her body is as thin as a swamp reed.
She rarely speaks. For a long time we thought she was
mute, until one day Kyle asked her to bring him his
boots and she said, quite articulately and with a practiced
servility, that she would be happy to.

She came to us mysteriously. We woke up one day
and she had curled up near our campfire during the night.
She never said where she had come from, and nobody
remembered her as being from our colony. Because she
is so attentive to Kyle, I shouldn't like her as much as
I do. But I do.

After the man had been settled onto a palette, Ratzi
helped me grind up some scrapings from the black base
of the unicorn horn I had cut off earlier. Working slowly,
knowing that even with time against me I had to take
care, I pounded the hard scrapings into a soft grainy
powder. Mixing it with water and my own special mixture of herbs I formed a poultice wrapped in the blue-
green leaves of the molochait tree.

The man still slept as I applied the poultice to his leg.
He woke finally while I was wrapping a bandage around
the poultice and his leg. Before focusing on me he looked
around the cave, taking in the cookfire where Ratzi still
stirred her stew; the racks of dried fish, salted meat, wild
vegetables; and the crates of equipment, guns, grenades,
bombs, etc. that we have stolen from the tincans' garrison and their ammo depots. When he did look at me,

he stared me right in the eye. For the first time in my life, I was a bit embarrassed by the way a man looked at me. I had read of maidenly blushes in my mother's books, but was somewhat ashamed to react so conventionally now.

"You're lovely," the man said.

"Please try not to move, pilot. You have been hurt."

"Don't I know it. My leg keeps sending reminders. Ouch, easy there."

"You'll feel better soon, I promise you."

"Okay, I'll accept your marker."

"My what?"

"Your marker. Sort of a document that records a promise."

"We can't possibly make a document. Paper's scarce. The only paper I have I use for my book."

"Your book?"

"I write down each of my days in a blank book I found. I record things in it."

"I see. Well, we don't really need paper for a proper marker. Your word'll do."

"You have my marker then. You'll be well soon."

When he smiled, his eyes seemed to light up a bit. He brushed away a falling lock of his light blond hair with his right hand. I felt funny, both pleased and uncomfortable at his friendly smile. The smile was not general, you see, it was specific. It was for me. And I was not ready for it.

"I'm beginning to remember. A meadow or something, looking up and seeing you and another person, a boy. . . ."

"That would be Kyle. Best not to call him a boy to his face. He likes to think of himself as a man."

"I understand. When I was his age I could create quite a fuss about just that. I thought I was a man at thirteen, until Gawr took me down a peg with the back of his good hand, the hand that was not a hook, thank God. I started feeling like a kid again then, I'll tell you."

"Gawr?"

"My father. Foster father, actually."

"Oh."

I did not like to talk about parents, so I said nothing about my own.

"Since you're working on saving my life, I'd like to know your name."

For a moment I did not want to tell him. The particular sensation I felt was too intense and complicated to explain here.

"Miri," I finally responded.

"Hello, Miri. I'm Starbuck."

"Good to meet you, Starbuck."

"Always glad to get formalities over with. Before, when I was being carried here, I woke up a couple of times. There were children. . . ."

"Yes. There are many. Sometimes as many as fifty, although from time to time a few disappear into the hills and don't return for some time. Right now there are less than forty in the band. . . ."

"Band? You guys are organized?"

"In a way. Most of the children have formed a band, an outlaw gang really. Kyle's their leader. I do not exactly approve of their actions. I do not belong."

"But you're with them now."

"I was concerned with rescuing you and tending to your injury. I had to engage Kyle's help."

"But you do not like Kyle very much."

"I like him. He's my brother. I just cannot join his group. I prefer to be an outsider."

"And Kyle is the leader of this, this gang of children?"

"Yes."

"But he's only a boy himself. I know, don't say it. He thinks of himself as a man. But he's really only a boy."

"That's true. However, he's the only leader the children have."

"Why do they need leaders? Where are the adults?"

"The colony dispersed when the tincans arrived. Some of the adults were captured, some were killed, others fled. Only Kyle and his band are left to fight the tincans."

"I'm not clear on all this. You said colony. Tell me about the colony."

"I don't want to go over ancient history."

"Ancient! How ancient can it be? You're only, what, sixteen, seventeen?"

I felt an irrational anger that he could so misjudge my age.

"I am eighteen," I said. "Do I look young for my age?"

"Well, you look good for your age, whatever it is, I'll say that. You're getting red. Flirting bothers you, does it?"

"A little."

"Don't worry. I'll try to curb the impulse, but I warn you, flirting is something of a habit with me, part of my nature. Please tell me about the colony."

I sighed. This Starbuck was a hard person to refuse.

"All right," I said.

I have not recorded much about our past in this book. I don't know if I can remedy that unfortunate omission readily. My mother has answered many of my questions and I have vague memories from my schooling, but my knowledge of history is probably a blend of misunderstood facts, exaggerated legends, and imagined events. I'm sure I want our history to be more attractive and more noteworthy than it is. I make this vow. I will find out more and record it in detail in another book—if I can ever find another source of paper.

Ours was a society of pariahs, outcasts forced to leave their homes and strike out on their own, escaping persecution by braving the hardships of an unknown planet. The original leaders of the pariahs are direct ancestors of myself and Kyle—and of Ariadne, Nilz, and Robus. In fact, the woman had the same name as our mother,

Megan. The first Megan and her husband (we've always
said husband and wife, although of course there are no
formal marriages in our society, and relationships do
shift from time to time) were both creative individuals
on the planet Scorpia. Marcsen was a writer who spec-
ialized in political allegories of an adversary nature.
Megan painted, using the type of Scorpion oils that, once
applied to canvas, could be adjusted in such respects as
color and texture by telepathic influence from the artist.
Only a few artists had the telepathic gift, and even fewer
could use it to influence the properties of Scorpion oils.
On Scorpia this ability was invaluable and very profit-
able. Even though Megan used her art, like Marcsen,
for political purposes, the government never moved
against her as it did the others. When the group was
ordered into exile, Megan was given the opportunity to
stay, subsidized by the government with a generous si-
necure. Government functionaries said right out that they
would not interfere with the political messages of her
paintings, that's how desperate they were for telepathic
art. Megan refused the offer, accepting instead the intense discomfort of a dilapidated freighter, crammed
with Marcsen and their fellow exiles into a cargo hold.
She produced some fine paintings after the colony was
established here on Antila, although some of her col-
leagues claimed that the vitality went out of her art when
its political content changed.

I know I have some telepathic ability. I communicate
with Rogue easily. Then again, maybe Rogue is just a
unicorn who transmits well. Still, once in a while, I pick
up a stray thought from Kyle or one of the children and,
though I don't attempt to verify it, I often find out I was
right about what they were thinking. But I am digressing
from this rather messy history of our colony.

The pariahs were political activists. Although they
concerned themselves with many and disparate social
issues in the bleak, cold, and emotionally remote world
of Scorpia, their main fight was against the war, a war

that had been raging nearly a thousand years even at that time. It was not their intention that the war should become the primary issue in what was essentially a social philosophy based on humanism and good works, but it was their opposition to war that the government chose to emphasize when it launched its campaign against them, a campaign that led eventually to their exile.

In truth, as Megan tells it (my mother Megan, that is), the pariahs were not specifically against the thousand year war. They regretted it, yes, but they understood some of the imperatives behind it. War was so much a fact of life for everyone in the twelve worlds that it was difficult to postulate alternatives to it. While the pariahs were pacifists who would not serve in the fighting forces, they did often go to war and serve on medical, food service, and clerical crews. Many of them died in Cylon attacks. What they were against on the home front was the set of militaristic attitudes that governed Scorpion society. And not only on Scorpia, for that matter—their ideas spread to the variously militaristic societies on all the twelve worlds. The increasing popularity of their ideas made them especially dangerous to the Scorpion government, which after its most recent elections (mere ceremonies really, because all opposition was squelched) had become even more warlike in its policies. So, higher levels decreed that the pariahs, who pointed out such obvious facts, had to be in some way silenced.

Fortunately, this was not a murderous government (in Scorpia's past, there had been many tyrannies based on the politics of assassination), and it chose first to harass its political opponents, then to persecute them, then to attract the most prosperous of the artists to work within the society in jobs that essentially defused their revolutionary artillery. When harassment, persecution, and economic temptations failed, exile was commanded by a narrow vote of the Scorpion legislative body. I wish I could be more specific about the mechanics of government on Scorpia, but political science is just not my strong point and the details of the history of that time remain a muddle to me. So Megan, Marcsen, and the others were transported to Antila in a space freighter so foul that about a quarter of their group died aboard ship from diseases and despair.

Antila proved only slightly more hospitable than the space freighter. The planet does have its beauties. There are areas where the vivid and provocative colors remind one, Megan says, of the kinds of effects created with Scorpion oils. On the other hand, Antila—with its wretched humidity, its tangled jungles, its poisonous forests, and its dangerous waters—brought more disease, more death. Until the colony's medical people devised immunizations for some of the most common diseases, the colony's population was further reduced. Additionally, they found that they could not wander far from their settlement (a settlement now inhabited and defiled by the ugly tincans for their garrison) because of the many predators that roamed the forests and jungles. Lions, leopards, wolves, plus many beasts for which there were no previous designations.

Not all Antilean animals were forbidding, however, and the survival of the colony can at least partly be attributed to the help received from the unicorns. There had been no unicorns on Scorpia, and so they were mysterious creatures to the colonists. They're mysterious creatures to everybody, always have been, always will be. No-one knows why the unicorns came voluntarily to the settlement. It was certainly not that they were a domesticable animal. No unicorn is ever domesticated. It becomes a steed for human riders by its own choice. Even now one of our unicorns, Magician, will not accept a human on its back, although it willingly pulls plows and picks fruit off the higher branches with its horn for us. Some say that unicorns are basically intelligent natives of Antila who have formed this symbiotic alliance with us as defense against the predators and the climate.

The unicorns, after all, are not exactly thriving here either.

Some unicorns are able to link with humans telepathically, as with myself and Rogue. (Sometimes I think Magician communicates with me, but when I turn toward him and flash a thought back he becomes aloof, pointing his elegant horn straight upward, and he pretends he has transmitted nothing.) People like Kyle say the telepathic link between human and unicorn is imagined, and does not exist at all. They are just animals, he says, and like all good animals they respond to human signals, and what seems like an exchange of thought is accomplished through physical movements and gestures rather than through the minds of human and unicorn. I gave up arguing with him on that subject long ago. I prefer not to argue with him at all if I can. He's repulsive when he loses his temper. His blue eyes go gray, and his crooked nose wrinkles and adds another bump, and his mouth becomes a twisted piece of metal. It's best to leave him alone, let him enjoy his game of leadership, and look for ways to fix his mistakes and correct his miscalculations when they occur.

The pariah colony finally got through their initial difficulties and set up a society based on the ethical principles that had precipitated their exile. My Megan says that the Megan of that time, always the iconoclast, spoke against the way the colonists were establishing their society. She was alone in her protests. Even her husband Marcsen turned against her, and their marriage ended by mutual agreement. She never took up with any other man or woman. Her argument with the colony was that the ethical principles were fine but not enough to hold a government together. One should venerate ethics and strive for ethical behavior, but a society must be built on firmer foundations, she believed. They could not, for example, just throw together a constitution that said, in effect, that everyone must treat one another according to a rather restricted though humanistic set of ideas. There must be more practical approaches, she claimed. Every man cannot be a legislator, she said, any more than every man can be a king.

Well, talk like that got her nowhere except for a sort of exile among her own people. She retired to her cottage to paint pictures with her last remaining Scorpion oils. These last paintings are magnificent. They are hidden, along with other hastily-preserved art works in the passage I use to visit my mother, my Megan, in the garrison prison. Among the earlier Megan's paintings, I have a particular favorite. It shows a woman dressed in a gown that has many telepathically created shades of purple in it. (The real advantage of telepathic art is that colors you can imagine but cannot mix are possible.) The woman is sitting in a leisurely fashion on a unicorn. The animal is so fully textured you think, if you touch the canvas, you will feel real hair on the unicorn's side, and that some of it will be matted from the heat. You think you could pull at the thick tufts of hair around its hooves. It is a sort of blue-white unicorn and the blue and white shades change easily with a change of light. Behind the unicorn and the woman (she is not an extraordinarily beautiful woman, as one finds in the more sentimental art of the colony's later period, the period of political and social decline, but she is angularly attractive, something like my Megan) is a dense jungle scene in which you can see hints of lions, wolves, other animals. On some visits to the passage I think I see a bird on a particular branch, then it isn't there the next time I view it.

To get back to the original Megan, she died while the society was still smug and self-satisfied about its apparent success. She probably thought she had been mistaken, that a society based solely on advanced ethical principles could survive just fine. The deterioration came after her death. Corruption, petty crimes, more than petty crimes, and—above everything else—a substitution of selfishness (a kind of take-what-you-want-because-it-might-never-come-your-way-again philosophy) for the original idealism reduced the colony to a sorry state. Even then it might have saved itself. My mother and father, Megan and Renkin, were making headway in a revision of the colony's laws. Their revisions would have initiated a system based on the original Megan's beliefs. But then the disaster came. The tincans. We had no reason to expect them. We kept no skywatches. And, anyway, we were off in a corner of the so-called civilized universe. Antila has no military value as an outpost and there are thousands of other planets with better resources. The climate here is bad for the tincans. They died almost as frequently as our original colonists. But I guess death is no problem for the tincans, who are dispensers of death, after all. And their impulse for conquest apparently includes even unexploitable and valueless planets.

So the tincans came and the colony was finished. Some colonists escaped and are hiding in the distant hills, satisfied to scrounge like rats for their daily existence and happy that tincan patrols never bother with them. Some, Kyle's band of children, inhabit the jungle around the garrison and attack the tincans whenever they can. And some, like my mother (my father was murdered by the tincans, but I have never described his death in this book, and will not. Ever.) are captives of the tincans, kept in a damp darkness and declining gradually in health and spirits.

CHAPTER SIX

Ratzi kept forcing spoonsful of stew on Starbuck while he listened to Miri's calmly-related history of the Antilean colony. The stew tasted vaguely sweet, as if there were a trace of fruit in it. The pain in his leg was subsiding; its throbbing had become irregular. From time to time he glanced down at the poultice, wondered what magical potion was contained beneath those bandage wrappings of blue-green triangular leaves.

The colony's history interested and perplexed Starbuck. At first he regretted the oppression of the Scorpion government, but then the Scorpions were notorious even among the Galactican fleet survivors for their eager support of oppressive measures and their volatile temperaments when things did not go their way. What Miri said about the repression of thought in all the twelve colonies was simply not supported by fact. On Caprica, Starbuck's home planet, the government had not been particularly militaristic in its ways. Nor was the society repressive. Yet, he recalled, he grew up thinking almost exclusively about the war and the part he would play in it, so perhaps the state control was more subtle on Caprica. Still, Caprica would not have sent this group of pariahs in a wretched freighter to a hostile environment, he was certain of that. Whatever else might be said, Caprica was definitely not Scorpia.

He also could not avoid noticing the correspondences between the Antilean colony and the peaceful river settlement of his second therapy room fantasy. I wonder, he thought, if there are always hidden threats to any apparently peaceful society, even for people as idealistic as the Antilean pariahs. Did humans in groups always threaten their own well-being by such splits into factions, and the inability to hold firm to their best thoughts, their most attractive ideals? Or did this group simply fail, not so much because of its beliefs, but because the nature of human progress was not in maintaining a rigid adherence to delimited philosophies but instead in a successful response to change.

Starbuck's reflections on Miri's telling of the history, together with the warm food and especially the numbing of his pain, relaxed him so much that he drifted gently off to sleep, just as Miri was beginning to describe the Cylon invasion of Antila. He dreamt of his childhood. In it he was about eight or nine. He was crouched behind a rock, his attention riveted on a toy instrument panel. Not far from the rock his scale-model viper flew toward the model of a Cylon raider, which was being operated by a friend who himself was hiding somewhere near. The friend, like all children who played this game, did not like to take the part of a Cylon, but somebody had to be the enemy when you played vipers and raiders. It was truly more fun to be the controller of the viper, since—in addition to the superior maneuverability of even a toy viper—you also had the psychological advantage over the already dissatisfied manipulator of the enemy craft. As the two models approached each other, Starbuck abruptly plunged his into a quick turn and short dive. He intended to come up on the raider from beneath and try for a direct hit lowside. But his playmate anticipated the move and set the raider into a modified pinwheel spin. Starbuck awaited the raider's emergence from the spin, and he pressed the button on the miniature joystick of his toy panel to fire a shot. He was too eager and missed the raider by a mile. That was all right, he could line it up easy for the second volley. But there was no second volley. Starbuck almost always got in two bursts of laser fire before a playmate could get off his first shot, but this time his playmate showed extraordinarily quick reaction time, and a beam from the raider split the viper in half. The viper dropped into tall grass and, for a moment, the mock-fire flared. All systems on his panel clicked off with a flash of light and a low grumble. The child Starbuck had always resented losing, but he had to congratulate the playmate. As was his custom when he was eight or nine, he leapfrogged over the rock that had concealed him. Climbing out from under a bush on the other side of the playing field was his playmate. But it was no-one Starbuck remembered from his childhood. No, but he knew him. It was Kyle, looking arrogantly triumphant and ready to continue the battle with bare fists.

He came awake suddenly, expecting to see Kyle starting a swing at him. But nothing inside the cave chamber had changed. Ratzi was still sitting beside him silently, spoon in stewpot. And Miri was still standing near the cookfire. The fire was dwindling to ash, but that was the only difference.

"Was I sleeping long?"

"Not long. Probably long enough to help your leg get better."

He stretched the leg. Amazingly, there was little pain left, just a twinge when the leg was held straight out.

"You cured me. How'd you do it?"

Miri shrugged.

"A little powder changed into a paste. I don't know any names for it. I've always been able to do it. Megan says I'm gifted that way."

"Megan?"

"My mother. She's—"

"Dead," Kyle said, striding into the room. "Our mother is dead. She was killed along with our father when the tincans came and responded to our flags of truce with artillery fire. The tincans killed many of us before we were finally subdued."

Miri seemed about to protest but her mouth hardened

into a firm line. Starbuck wondered what she was holding
back.

"You don't seem so subdued," Starbuck said. "You
all seem to be surviving very well, for children."

Kyle's voice broke as he shouted:

"We are not children!"

Starbuck knew he should be amused by this adolescent's posturings, but instead he was angry in return.

"What are you then, all you eight and ten and fourteen
year olds, if you're not children?"

"We are warriors!"

Starbuck laughed, and that laugh did more to infuriate
Kyle than any words could. For a moment his arms
flailed and he could not speak. Ratzi ran to him and
touched his arm, but he pushed her away. She stayed
slightly behind him, ready to help if he ever acknowl-
edged a need. Miri watched Kyle's anger passively.

"I knew you would not understand," Kyle said.
"We've been robbed of any sense of childhood. We are
at war, that makes us warriors."

Starbuck's anger immediately left him at these words.
Proclaiming his adulthood, Kyle seemed more a child
than ever.

"All right, I get your drift. But your thinking's dangerous, Kyle, for yourself and for the others. Even if
you're right and *you* have somehow achieved manhood
prematurely, *they're* just children—little boys and girls.
But not young warriors!"

"That *is* what we are, lieutenant, just as you say,
young warriors."

"You do speak like a leader, Kyle, I'll give you that.
But don't you see how you are endangering the oth—
the children. *They* can be killed or captured."

Kyle laughed, a bit too proudly for Starbuck's taste.

"We are too swift," the young leader said. "Our attacks too precise, too well-timed, too well-planned."

Starbuck was surprised.

"*You* attack *them*?"

"They are the enemy," Kyle said laconically. "They took all we ever had, set up their station in our settlement, killed many of our parents. So now we hurt them. We strike at their ammunition depots, fuel dumps, patrols. We saved you from one of their patrols today, lieutenant."

"And I thank you for it. But—"

Starbuck stopped, realizing that anything he could say would only antagonize Kyle further. The young man's defiant stare made him uneasy and, although his leg was without pain now, he was feeling too exhausted to argue.

Two children, twins from the look of them, rushed into the cave and announced that a tincan patrol had been diverted from pursuit with a false trail the twins had laid down. Kyle crisply thanked them for their report, then apologized to Starbuck for the laxity of discipline in their demeanor. Starbuck said he thought they were quite disciplined—for their age. Kyle glared at him, then muttered he had his duty to attend to (placing special emphasis on the word *duty*), and he left the cave chamber, his raised shoulders clearly displaying the immense anger he was holding in. Seeing the wound to Kyle's pride, Starbuck immediately regretted the sarcasm of his remark.

CHAPTER SEVEN

FROM MIRI'S BOOK:

Starbuck watched Kyle go. When he looked back at me, there was a hint of sadness in his eyes.

"You'll have to excuse Kyle," I said. "He thinks he's so, well, grown up since he's had to assume responsibility for the other children."

"I shouldn't have been so hard on him."

"Nobody's been hard on him for a good long time. It might just do him some good."

Ratzi offered Starbuck another spoonful of food. He waved it away. Ratzi's reaction was disappointment, as it always was when someone refused her help. She needs to serve. I've tried to argue her out of it, make her a bit more independent, but I soon realized that she was not happy unless what she did had a clear benefit to someone else. Especially Kyle—although our newcomer seemed to have immediately charmed her, too.

"I'm stuffed," Starbuck, observing her pout, said. "Really. I didn't realize how hungry I was. It's good. Really."

His praise satisfied Ratzi. She carried the bowl away with the pride of a soldier just awarded a distinguished service medallion.

Starbuck gestured toward the high pile of books against the near wall.

"Who reads?" he asked.

"We all do. Books and paper are prime commodities on Antila. Quite scarce at the moment, although the tincans have a room full of unused paper in their garrison. I stole some of it for my book that last time I—"

I stopped talking abruptly, wondering what it was about Starbuck that made me so chatty. I didn't usually give away secrets that easily. Not even Kyle knew about the storeroom of paper. I wanted to keep that discovery to myself for the time being, not let anyone find out I hoarded paper in order to record my secret thoughts. A vain project, perhaps—vain both in the sense of futility and vanity—but, if Kyle ever does need paper, I'll give him some. He has this odd passion for writing cryptic messages on oilskin, anyway.

I also doubted that Kyle would want me to inform Starbuck about the secret passage into the garrison, either. He had already, after all, told Starbuck that Megan was dead, when in fact she was in the tincans' prison. I sneak into the garrison regularly to see her.

"I can tell there's something you don't wish to talk about," Starbuck said gently.

I nodded.

"Well, I won't ask then. But about the books, you say you all read them?"

"Except for a couple of the youngest children who aren't ready yet. They choose war games over education."

"You sound bitter."

"I am, a bit. I want them to have some knowledge, something else to understand besides the ways of this awful planet, and the details of warfare. Most of Kyle's band feel they don't need any education, but Kyle forces them to attend my classes as part of their routine duty."

"Classes? You're their teacher then?"

I felt myself blushing, because he seemed so impressed with that small feat.

"I do my best," I said.

"I always like to meet a woman as long on brains as she is on beauty."

Now my face was really red, I was sure. And for two reasons. First, because I am as susceptible to glib flattery from a handsome male as anybody but, second, because

of the veiled insult to women attached to the compliment.
At that moment he seemed as arrogant as Kyle when
Kyle boasts about male superiority. I always rankle at
Kyle and, for a moment, I felt a similar anger at Starbuck.
Yet, the grin that went with the words was ingratiating,
and I thought that he simply might be trying to please
his nurse. Men are like that sometimes, Megan told me—
when they are sick, it becomes the primary goal in their
life to please the nurse. I decided not be angry with him.
I liked him so much, anyway, it would have disturbed
me to fight him.

"So," I said, trying to be as matter-of-fact as I could,
"you think I'm pretty?"

"Miri, when you arrive on the *Galactica*, you'll have
suitors galore."

I started to say that 'suitors galore' was not my idea
of a worthwhile goal, when I realized *all* of what he'd
just said.

"Back on the *Galactica*?" I said, shocked.

"You can't stay here. You and Kyle and the whole
band of children, we'll get you off this backwater ugly
planet. It's the best thing. Especially with your parents,
well, gone and the settlement in shambles, as it will be
after I take charge and we make the attack on it, myself
and whoever comes to rescue me. The children can just
retire from warfare as of now. There'll be no reason
to—"

"Wait a minute, wait," I cried. "You're talking too
fast. We can't go!"

"And just why not?"

I could not answer without divulging information that
Kyle wanted kept from him—about Megan and all.

"I can't tell you now," I said weakly.

I didn't know what to do. I would have to sneak into
the tincans' garrison again. I *had* to talk with Megan.

CHAPTER EIGHT

Spectre was so furious that he considered scrapping the entire mud-splattered patrol.

"Did I hear right?" he said to its leader. "You were *all* sprawled on the ground, pushed there by a mob of little children, and you could not get off a single good shot?"

"Yes, honored commander sir," said the leader. When one of Spectre's minions appended the *honored* to his automatic response, it was clear he was apprehensive. And Spectre had disassembled warriors for smaller mistakes than this.

"And the pilot escaped."

"We are tracking the guerillas, but you know how effectively they lay down false trails, sir."

Angrily, Spectre dismissed the patrol and told Hilltop to send out another search party immediately. Hilltop announced that the new patrol had already been formed and dispatched. Spectre was impressed. This Hilltop was proving to be a fine aide, a very fine aide. He might shift him from temporary to permanent duty.

His consideration of Hilltop's promotion was rudely interrupted by the sudden sound of an explosion outside the garrison walls. The floors of his office rocked with tremors. Rushing outside, he saw that a part of the original fuel dump was in flames. Hilltop, his outfit gleaming from reflected fire, sped forward, demanding explanations for the explosion and fire. When he had received them, in addition to a sealed packet handed Hilltop by a centurion, he reported back to Spectre:

"Fuel dump sabotaged, sir."

"The children?"

"Yes, so it appears. They left this packet behind, actually threw it to one of our warriors."

Hilltop gave Spectre the packet, which Spectre carried back to his office before inspecting it. Inside the animal-skin wrappings was a rolled-up oilskin.

"A message, Hilltop. For the first time the children's army is communicating with us."

"Perhaps they offer peace, sir, a truce."

Spectre perused the message.

"No, I'm afraid it's hardly a matter of peace, unless double-cross has become a pacifistic strategy. But this is better than a truce, Hilltop. It is an offer that we can turn to our advantage. Come with me."

"May I ask our destination, sir?" Hilltop said, as he struggled to keep up with his fast-gliding commander.

"The prison, Hilltop. Our business is at the prison. I must talk with one of the humans there. One Megan, do you know anything about her?"

"Wasn't she a leader of the colony here?"

"One of the fiercest, Hilltop. I've been trying to break her for some time. If you humiliate their leaders, you reduce the courage of your enemies. I have never been able to humiliate Megan. She is sick and weak. She can hardly talk. But, in her weakest voice, she is still defiant. It will be a pleasure to observe this final humiliation."

They reached the prison, a grain silo before the Cylon takeover. The prisoners were kept in some makeshift cells in the silo's upper reaches. They had named their prison *the tower*. All of its windows were covered over, and even Spectre felt a hint of gloom when he entered its bleak dark interior.

CHAPTER NINE

Getting to Megan proved more difficult than I'd anticipated. When I left Starbuck, I found Kyle at the mouth
of the cave, standing stiffly in one of his proud-leader
poses, no doubt conscious of the impressive figure he
cut in the varying light filtering through the waterfall.
He was discussing strategy with his two chief aides (the
oldest of the children), Herbert the Singer and Jergin.
Herbert the Singer, although blessed with a sweet tenor
voice and a knowledge of—it seems—every song ever
composed, is otherwise not one of my favorite people.
Every time I glance at him he seems to be indulging in
another of his odd habits—picking tiny insects out of his
hair or scratching his ankles to the bone. Jergin, on the
other hand, is quite possibly the loveliest girl in the entire
outlaw band, and her cheerfulness often builds up our
spirits.

A report had come in from observers sent to the settlement area that the tincans were busily moving materials from the fuel dump to piles inside the garrison.
Kyle ordered that we send in the smallest children to the
remaining section of the dump and plant some timed
explosive charges there, right under the tincans' noses.
I protested, said he couldn't risk their lives that way. It
was too callous. He glanced at me oddly, a bit smugly
I thought, and said I had never objected before when he
sent out *any* of the children on *any* mission. Then he
ignored me pointedly and, in that deep growl of leadership voice he used around his aides, he gave the rest

of the orders. I volunteered to accompany the mission team, hoping that I could slip away from it and into the secret passage, whose entrance was beneath a false bush not far from the fuel dump area.

But I wasn't able to reach the passageway entrance.

I watched the group of our four smallest children, including my brothers Nilz and Robus, slither their way through the platoon of tincans working around the fuel dump, then plant the explosives (explosives, incidentally, which we had stolen from the tincans' supplies on earlier raids). After they had slithered their way back to us, Kyle whispered the countdown for the timed charges, which went off right on schedule. The explosion itself was spectacular. Licks of fire topped the tall trees. Flames slithered along the ground in a way that reminded me of the children's earlier movements. After making sure that the explosion had destroyed an impressive amount of material, Kyle called for retreat. I split away from the group and made for the secret entrance. Unfortunately, the explosion had thrown some debris too near the entrance and there were tincans already engaged in clearing the area. I knew there was no sense in trying the passageway right then and, if I waited too long for the tincans to leave, Kyle would notice my absence and get in a snit about it, so I returned to camp with the mission squad.

Starbuck had been moved from the cave to the camp at Kyle's orders. He was walking almost normally, with only a slight limp.

"Well," Kyle said, "you look fit, lieutenant."

"Whatever Miri put on my leg, it's working. I picked up a leg wound in a fracas on a planet called Kobol not long ago, and, even with the help of the *Galactica* medical team, I didn't improve this fast." He turned toward me, smiled. "Thank you, Miri."

And, damn it, I blushed again.

"We have been busy," Kyle said.

"Yes," said Starbuck, "I heard the big explosion.

Ratzi told me what you guys were up to. You accomplished your objective?"

"Yes, lieutenant."

"Well, congratulations. I guess."

I would have thought that Kyle would puff up with pride at a genuine colonial starfleet warrior's approval, but his sidelong look at Starbuck was guarded, and he muttered sullenly:

"Thanks, lieutenant."

At that time I should have sensed that Kyle was planning something underhanded, but I was so intent on my own obsessions, my odd feelings for Starbuck and my need to consult Megan, that I missed the signs that he was hiding something.

"Feel up to riding, lieutenant?" Kyle asked, his voice close to friendly. "There might be another mission soon, and you might be useful to it."

"Well, I don't know about missions, but I can ride."

Kyle seemed a bit miffed that Starbuck displayed some reluctance to his offer, but he remained polite to him. I should have seen that as an omen, too. Kyle's almost never polite.

"Do you have a mount for me?" Starbuck asked.

"We have only one steed available at the moment. His name is Magician."

I'm sure my mouth dropped open a foot.

"Magician?!" I shouted. "But Kyle—"

"Miri," Kyle said harshly. "This isn't your affair. You mustn't spook the lieutenant. I'm sure he and Magician will get along together fine."

"Kyle!"

I made his name into two syllables, as I always do when I'm maddeningly angry at him. Starbuck started to laugh.

"Let's not have any sibling rivalry here. I gather from Miri's response that this Magician isn't exactly the gentlest creature around here."

Kyle, taken aback some by the lieutenant's accurate

perception, waited a couple of beats before answering:

"Magician is, well, just a tad temperamental. He is all we have for you to ride. However, if you *can't* handle him, then I'll lend you my steed, Demon, and ride Magician myself."

What a boastful bluff! Kyle had often tried to ride Magician in the past and, each time, the unicorn gently but firmly threw him off his back. I could see Kyle's game. He wanted to humiliate Starbuck, so that the combat-experienced warrior wouldn't be tempted to take over leadership. I could have told Kyle that Starbuck was not such a threat, any fool could see that.

"Where is this Magician?" Starbuck asked.

Kyle pointed. Magician stood near the command tent, one of his hooves jerkily pawing at the ground, making a series of uneven ovals in the dirt. He didn't look friendly.

Starbuck went up to him, slowly walked around him, touched him on the nose.

"Magician, hey? Not long ago, in a dream, I rode a black, sleek, and beautiful horse like Magician."

"This isn't a dream, lieutenant," Kyle said sneeringly.

"Well, Magician, are you going to allow me to ride you?" Starbuck whispered, his mouth close to Magician's ear.

Kyle made a scoffing sound in his throat; he obviously felt his ploy would work. Then the most extraordinary thing happened. Magician's head nodded ever so slightly. Starbuck laughed and turned toward us, looking quite pleased.

"I could swear I just heard this animal say it'd be all right with him. It'd be all right with him for me to ride him."

"But Magician's never allowed any—"

Before Kyle could complete his protest, Starbuck had smoothly swung himself onto the black unicorn's back. There was a long nervous pause as Kyle and I and the children stared at Starbuck, who sat quite relaxed atop

Magician. I expected Magician to rear up and cast Starbuck away at any second. Instead, he glanced toward
Kyle and trotted a few steps with Starbuck firmly remaining on his back.

"This is weird," Starbuck remarked, "but I do believe
he sort of welcomed me aboard."

Kyle looked ready to drop his pants and kiss his ankles. I laughed. I had heard the same message from
Magician in my own head. Kyle, as untelepathic as ever,
had of course heard nothing.

"He likes you, Starbuck," I hollered. "Magician's
telepathic, you're the first one to ride him, and he likes
you."

Then, pleased by Kyle's embarrassment, I laughed
all the harder. Starbuck whispered to Magician, who
seemed to nod, then took his rider on a fast gallop around
the periphery of the camp. Magician's head was held
high, and Starbuck rode him as if, simply, he'd always
rode him. When he told me later that he'd hardly ever
ridden any kind of animal, I couldn't believe him. No
tenderfoot could have ridden Magician.

Kyle disguised his jealousy well. He watched impas-
sively as his little band became more and more infatuated
with our pilot from a distant battlestar. When Starbuck
had finished his ride on Magician, the Genie performed
the best of her magic tricks with more flourishes than
usual. He said her sleight-of-hand was masterful, and
he himself was a master so he should know. The Genie,
usually magical and mysterious herself, positively glowed
with pleasure. Melysa and Chubby Marta did one of their
quaint folkdances which they claim they reconstructed
from ballet archives kept by the adults in the hills. Herbert the Singer gave Starbuck a rendition of a mournful
dirge recounting the slaughter of our colonists by the
tincans. As usual, the song brought a tear or two even

to Kyle's eyes. Goodchild and Arno Armwaver fought each other over who could be Starbuck's servant and valet. Starbuck settled the dispute by giving both of them the job, then said there were no duties attached. At first they were puzzled, then he told them such a position was generally considered honorary. They became puffed with pride. Even Ratzi reduced her attention toward Kyle to find ways to push more food on Starbuck than he actually required. Kyle observed all this without a hint of jealousy crossing his face. I should have realized that he had something up his sleeve, but I merely thought he had adjusted to the pilot's presence and popularity. I even believed he thought he could learn something useful from Starbuck's vast experience with warfare. God, I should have known better. Kyle passive is Kyle devious.

My need to see and talk with Megan kept me edgy. I knew if I sneaked away now, while the camp was in such an uproar of excitement over Starbuck, Kyle might suspect I was up to something, and send someone to follow me. I needed an excuse, so I asked Laughing Jake to accompany me on a foraging patrol, to look for curative herbs. Laughing Jake has an instinct for locating hard-to-find plants, and so the expedition had the appearance of being businesslike and logical. Jake was also loyal to me, and I could trust him to cover for me after we cleared camp and I went off on my own.

As soon as we were far enough away, I asked Jake to go searching for the herbs and to take a good long time in doing it. He nodded at me in his usual dolorous way. We call him Laughing Jake because he never does laugh, never even cracks a smile, and in fact his long narrow face makes him look ever more mournful than he is.

I left Rogue in a clump of trees at the edge of the clearing. He'd keep himself concealed, come at my call when I reemerged from the passage. This time there were no tin cans around the passage's entrance. They had cleared away the debris from the fuel dump explosion. The area did not even show that a fuel dump had once been there.

Checking to see that I was unobserved, I lifted the bush that covered the entrance and speedily slipped into the narrow hole that led to a small downward tunnel which in turn opened out into the main passage. I had left an electronic torch concealed in a chink behind a rock at the entranceway. After listening carefully to be sure nothing disturbed the quiet of the passage, I lit the torch and proceeded onward. The tunnel was as eerie as ever. Its rocky walls were so jagged that one could see any form one wished among its thousands of shadows. I could have sworn I saw an army of the enemy pressed against the wall and waiting to spring at me.

I passed the alcove where the art works are stored, each one in its heavy cloth wrappings to protect it as well as possible from the cloying underground dampness. This time I was so in haste I did not even stop to take the woman-unicorn painting of the original Megan's out of its wrappings for my regular viewing. I also passed chambers in which our library, records, and documents were kept. There was also an alcove containing medical supplies but, except for bandaging material and other small items, I never pilfered it for anything because I simply didn't have the proper medical knowledge. It's a pity there is not even a medic among the prisoners.

The passage's exit was through the back of a fireplace in a room which the tincan commander had turned into a warehouse of diverse supplies. This commander was a hoarder, no doubt about that. He had collected such surprising supplies as powdered food (which the tincans don't seem to require), epidermal massage creams (also unused), soap (unused), plant seeds (unused), metal polish (used, but enough boxes of it to make ten tincan armies dazzlingly shine), and who knows what other ridiculous items. I slid back the fireplace panel carefully. Occasionally one of the tincans was in the room, but so far none had ever spotted me emerging from the fireplace. This time the room was empty, and I crept around cartons and metal boxes to the warehouse doorway.

Opening the door a crack, I could see only a few tincans in the yard. One group was engaged in one of their silly jerky marches, others were cleaning guns, still others were doing things that apparently made sense only if you were a tincan.

This was the hard part of my journey. The courtyard which I had to cross to get to the prison tower was often heavily populated with tincans, sometimes too many of them for me to even make a try. I always had to take a roundabout route, clinging to walls, crouching behind the few low objects that afforded me some cover.

This time the crossing was easy. Never before have I seen so many of the tincans so intent on their duty. None of them even so much as looked up. Must be some kind of shakeup going on, I thought. When I reached the tower, I nudged its main door open a little ways to make sure none of the guards was near the door. Again, my luck held. The usual guards were in other parts of the prison. Carefully but hastily, I made my way up the narrow iron flight of stairs that led to the block of cells where my mother, along with several other survivors of the tincan invasion, was imprisoned. Fortunately, Megan was in the last cell of the row or I might have never been able to get to her. There was a little depression in the wall next to her cell where I could secrete myself from any passing guards.

Megan was standing at the rear of the cell, which she shared with three other prisoners. Two of them were asleep, the other looked dazed with insanity.

"Mother," I whispered.

She turned slowly and nodded. I was about to say something more, but suddenly I heard the clanking sounds on the iron stairway. Quickly I retreated into my tiny alcove, trying to make myself as small as possible.

I did take a peek out to see what was happening.

Approaching Megan's cell was the odd-looking commander of the tincans, a blue-robed figure with a metallic face who seemed to glide rather than walk. His name, I knew, was Spectre.

I huddled into the alcove as I heard Spectre call Megan's name. The lice-ridden rust-streaked lump of metal, what did he want with my mother?

CHAPTER TEN

Some time during the last couple of days focussing her eyes had become extremely difficult and painful. For Megan, that was something new. Her eyesight had always been good. Even though she had always been a voracious reader, she had never needed corrective lenses. She wondered now, however, if seeing everything blurrily really made any difference. What was there to look at? The only breaks in the monotony of the gray cell were the dirty yellow of the straw she and the other prisoners used for bedding, the blackness of the iron bars, and the occasional burst of light when one of the Cylons opened the entrance door two levels down.

Certain prisoners had tried to remove the boarding over their narrow silo windows. For a while it had least given them a cause but, of course, once the boarding had been pushed away (the prisoners cheered as they squeezed their heads through the small aperture and watched boards fall to the ground below), the Cylons came and replaced it. After two or three such attempts, the project had collapsed of its own futility.

There had once been a blue and yellow pattern in jagged stripes on Megan's tunic, but the filthiness of the cell had turned her clothing to gray also. Perhaps the present problem with her eyesight was a blessing. Blindness might just be preferable to this overwhelming grayness.

She ran her right hand through her thinning hair. A few gray strands stuck to her fingers. She had lost a lot of hair during her confinement, and she had no idea how she might now look. Marcsen, who had admired her hair

and loved to touch it, would probably cry if he were
alive to see her. On one of Miri's visits, Megan had
asked her whether her balding was obvious, did the scalp
show through, but Miri had dodged the question with
one of her clever urgent changes of subject.

As usual her head throbbed with that vague center-
of-the-forehead headache that had plagued her even before her confinement. She missed Miri's soothing touch.
A few strokes of her daughter's thin dainty fingers, up
and down the brow, rubbing steadily but gently, had
nearly always cured Megan's headaches. Miri had occasionally reached through the bars and stroked her
mother's forehead, but the remedy had never worked
well in this damnable damp cell, which created its own
pains. Now her stomach was unsettled by a dull pain,
too. That was at least explainable. Not only did the
Cylons serve the prisoners meager food portions, they
had not the slightest interest in how to prepare human
food. Some prisoners had volunteered for kitchen duty,
but Spectre said he saw no utility to that. Prisoners were
not supposed to eat well, he said, with that odd sneer
he could delicately infuse into his otherwise nasally
metallic voice. To complete her catalog of pain, her legs
were steadily weakening from an apparently arthritic
condition. She forced herself to walk around the perimeter of the cell several times a day. The exercise was
helping the ailment during the day, but the steady ache
during the nighttime hours disturbed her sleep.

She had just completed one of her regular walks when
she heard Miri's whisper. As she turned to walk to the
iron bars, on the other side of which her daughter stood,
a flash of light appeared behind Miri, followed by the
sounds of Cylons coming up the stairs. Miri scampered
to her alcove hiding place. Just in time, as it turned out,
for Spectre appeared on the cell block level, flanked by
two of his warriors.

"You've been neglecting me, Spectre," Megan said.
"I was beginning to feel rejected."

The commander, who—surprisingly enough—appreciated human irony, emitted a gurgling sound that Megan presumed indicated pleasure.

"I have had no use for you lately, Megan. Now I do."

"Oh? Why do you bother with me at all? I'll die long before you get anything useful out of me."

"I have realized that. So, I have decided to end my efforts with you."

"Termination?"

Megan inadvertently glanced toward Miri's hiding place, hoping that her daughter would not angrily reveal herself if it did prove that Spectre was here to oversee Megan's execution.

"Not termination at all. I am not a tyrant, Megan. No, I came here today to tell you, you will be freed. Tonight."

For a moment Megan could not speak. Spectre often surprised her, but this shock was the biggest yet. At first she felt irrationally pleased. Anything to get out of the cell—she needed freedom, needed to be reunited with her children, needed to find ways to oppose these invaders. But that was foolish thinking, all of it. This Spectre would not free her without some execrable secret motive. Spectre would only offer a deal with strings attached, enough strings to girdle Antila's equator. Therefore, her reply was wary:

"Freed? You said freed?"

"Yes, I received this just moments ago. It was secretly placed at our gate while . . . while a diversion of sorts was occurring."

"I believe I felt the tremors of that . . . diversion of sorts, Spectre."

Spectre held out an oilskin and carefully slipped it between the bars of the door. Megan accepted it hesitantly, afraid it might be concealing a bomb or be treated with a skin poison. When it proved to be a normal unsabotaged oilskin, she unrolled it and read the message. The neat structured printing was definitely Kyle's.

"We have the colonial warrior your patrols are searching for so clumsily. We will exchange him for your prisoner Megan after sunset tonight at Wolf Point, where the river's rapids become calm. We will wait on the north side of the river, your party will arrive from the south. Before you arrive, sound the usual signal. Place Megan on a raft and send her to us. At the same moment we will place a raft holding the pilot onto the river from our side. The signal to launch rafts will be three short blasts of our horn. If you double cross us, our revenge will be awesome. Kyle."

Tears flowed freely from Megan's eyes as she read the message.

"Lord, no!" she whispered. "What does he think he's doing?"

"It should be obvious," Spectre said. "Like all good loving children, he wishes his mother back. Fortunately it is possible. I would say that this offer of trade is shrewd, perhaps the most intelligent thing he can do."

Megan violently threw the oilskin at the iron door. It hit a point on the bars just in front of Spectre's face. She wished it had struck Spectre, even though he no doubt had no circuit for pain. He clearly had no circuit for flinching. A guard reached through the bars and retrieved the oilskin from the gray floor.

"You think I'm a bloody fool, is that it?" Megan hollered at Spectre. "You think you can hoodwink me into accepting this deal. Work on motherlove. Use my affection to make me come willingly to Wolf Point. Well, I don't believe you. I don't believe you'll ever go through with this trade, Spectre."

"What you believe is irrelevant. However it may surprise you to hear it, I do intend to go through with the trade. That pilot has a certain . . . value to me. A value superior to your utility to me, if your overwhelming sense of your own importance can allow you to accept that. I want the pilot, you may go free. The trade will occur but only . . . only if you cooperate with me in a matter that—"

"I should have known there was a catch. Of course. And if I don't cooperate with you?"

"Then I vow to slaughter your son, your other offspring, and their whole band of dirty renegade children at the exchange site and wherever else I may locate them."

Megan laughed.

"That's an empty boast. You haven't been able to catch them yet, and you've been scouring the forest for them desperately. Kyle and the other children're too smart for you."

"Is that so? Your Kyle proposed the trade. I would say it is he who is getting desperate."

Megan had to admit to herself the possibility of Spectre's claim. Kyle was so young. It was wrong for him and the other children to continue waging guerilla warfare when they should be—they should be—her head hurt so much she could not even pursue her thoughts to their natural conclusions. She must get rid of these Cylons so she could talk to Miri.

"So you think he's getting desperate? Why tell me that, Spectre? *If* you are going through with this exchange, you can do it without consulting me. Just do it!"

"I would like to, but . . ."

"There's always a *but* with you, Spectre. Out with it."

"I want your word that, once reunited with your family, you will take them away from this area. Join the refugees in the hills. Stay out of danger. I want you to tell Kyle to stop these senseless harassing attacks and vacate the immediate area."

Megan realized that the attacks could hardly be senseless and must be more than mere harassment if Spectre was so eager to go this far to stop them. No, he was hurting. He was clearly ineffective in coping with the gang of children, and it would not do for an ambitious wretch like Spectre to be ineffective. It might even short circuit his programming.

"You'd take my word?" she asked.

She thought she heard a satisfied hum pulsing beneath Spectre's words:

"I have come to learn that the word of some humanoids are binding. Once given, they are stronger than the strongest metal chain. You are such a human, Megan. You are tough and your word is trustworthy."

God, this machine could lay it on as thick as a Scorpion bricklayer, she thought. Her word was good, it was true, when given to another of her species. Why should he believe it was so binding with a nonhuman enemy? Well, better to go along with him.

"What about this pilot? What are your intentions with him?"

"That is not your concern."

But it *was* her concern. Who could even suspect what torture Spectre might have in store for the trapped warrior? It would be better for the trade not to take place, or for Kyle to work out a trick—but what? There was no time to work out such matters now.

"Do I have your word?" Spectre asked.

For a moment she contemplated defying him, but nothing was gained by rejecting the plan outright. Perhaps she could work with it.

She nodded her agreement, trying to appear as defeated as possible. Spectre, in his own mechanical way, seemed pleased.

"Excellent," he said. "We will arrange to travel to the site. We shall leave just before sunset. I will see that you have clean garments. I would not want your children to be . . . distressed by your appearance."

Spectre gestured to his guards. He glided to the top of the stairway, where they picked him up to carry him down. When he was out of sight, and the outside door had clanged shut, Miri slipped out from her hiding place, a look of perplexed puzzlement on her face.

"What was that all about?" Miri asked.

Megan told her daughter the details of Kyle's message.

"That fool!" Miri muttered. "He knows better than to trust the tincans."

Megan leaned closer to Miri, her pale hands clutching the iron bars.

"Tell him that, Miri. Tell him I said he should not go through with the exchange."

Miri's silence was definitely suspicious.

"What's wrong, daughter?"

"It's Kyle. He never believes I come here to see you. Whenever I tell him anything, he says I'm making it up. He doesn't trust me."

"You have to make him believe this time. You have to try, Miri. I cannot allow even a warrior to take my place."

"You're a fool, Megan!" came a deep voice from one of the straw beds. One of the sleepers, a former colony councilman named Kordel, had awakened. He had obviously overheard everything. Megan had never liked Kordel. He had always been a bit too prosperous, a bit too smug.

"Why do you care about a colonial warrior, Megan?" Kordel muttered. "He represents everything we were against, everything that caused our exile from Scorpia. He's a walking war machine, just like these filthy Cylons. What difference does it make? Make the exchange. Make it, return to your children, and run to the hills. The rest of us'd do it. There's no point in dying here."

Kordel's words were like a message from her own subconscious. Of course she had been considering it as a real possibility, considering her freedom, her reunion with her family, an escape from the Cylons. But she could not sacrifice another human being for any of that, even a warmongering starfleet warrior.

"No, I can't do that," she whispered to Kordel. "There

is a point in dying here. It's running away that has no point. Go to Kyle, Miri. Do what you can."

"Mother . . ."

"Do it."

There were tears in Miri's eyes. She said no more, and instead walked stealthily to the stairway, looked down, and in a moment had vanished into the gray darkness.

Megan almost cried. She wanted to hold her daughter close to her again, without the iron bars in the way. If she could only choose the exchange, the opportunity for that embrace was close, tempting. Why couldn't she be selfish, put her own cares and wishes first, especially in place of a man whose life represented the antithesis of her beliefs? Kordel would have not given the exchange a second thought. Even now he stared at her in disgust.

The ache in her head throbbed harder and the growing pain in her legs made it necessary for her to sit. She pulled at the cloth of her filthy prison garment. A piece of it broke off like ripped paper.

At least for a while she might have the feel of fresh new clothes on her ravaged body.

CHAPTER ELEVEN

FROM MIRI'S BOOK:
Mother's face haunted me as I made way back down the iron staircase, flitted from shadow to shadow in the courtyard, and slipped through the fireplace entrance into the secret passage. She had looked so haggard, so drawn. Her eyes, even when she wasn't angry at me, were bulging. They were as round as globes. And she didn't seem to blink. I could see by the odd way she held her body, straight but not quite straight enough, that she was in terrible pain. How could I allow her to go on in such pain? How could I allow her to remain in that wretched prison cell? I didn't have to. All I had to do was leave Kyle alone, let him trade Starbuck, disobey mother. Why not? As Kordel had said, Starbuck was a warrior, he knew the consequences of his actions. It was the duty of a soldier to lay down his life if necessary. Whatever she said, that was definitely *not* Megan's duty.

I was confused, my head in an absolute muddle. I wanted to save Megan, but I had been told by her to prevent the trade that would save her. At the same time, I wanted to save Starbuck, didn't want Kyle to go through with his plan. Yet I was willing to look the other way, let Kyle get away with this double-cross. And what, I wondered, was in Kyle's mind. Did he really think the trade, even if it brought back our mother, was a properly heroic act? Did it fit his overblown image of himself as the leader of an army?

Alone in the secret empty passage, I felt like screaming. There was no simple answer, no revelation of logic that would miraculously allow to occur all I really wanted—to have mother back without sacrificing Starbuck, without Kyle making such a repulsive fool of himself. There was no way, it seemed, I could straighten out my world.

I passed the alcove hideaway where the colony's art works were secreted. I was not going to go in, then I felt compelled to. The picture was there, still covered. As usual, I undid the wrappings and stared for a long while at the peaceful woman on the benign unicorn, at the beautiful but threatening jungle in the background, at the bird on the branch that, on this viewing, was present. Was there an answer in a beautiful work of art like this? I thought. If Megan was to be restored and look like the woman in the painting, would everything else miraculously right itself? The colony reunited, the ideal life again striven for, the people at peace? I laughed to myself. No, I thought, there'd always be the jungle, the hidden predators. At the same time, there'd always be the lovely birds and the beautiful trees. You could have everything, but you could not just cut out that one little part of the overall picture that you wanted. You couldn't close your eyes and pretend that evil did not exist. You might not be able to fight it, you might not choose to fight it, but you had to admit its existence.

I carefully replaced the painting in its wrappings and returned to the passage.

I had to try what Megan asked. But trying was the best I could do.

As I slipped out from the bush that concealed the outside entrance, I saw that the tincans milled about just inside the garrison walls. They were busy. Preparing for the exchange of prisoners, no doubt. I recalled Megan's horrifying physical weakness, and I hoped that the tincans would not push her too hard, crossing the expanse of jungle that led to Wolf Point. I did not like to think of her suffering any further.

I summoned Rogue and we headed back toward camp. We came to a rise that overlooked the trail to Wolf Point, and saw that Kyle's and his band had already set out on their mission. They rode single-file along the wide path. As usual Kyle, on Demon, led the way. Starbuck rode Magician, not far behind Kyle. It was clear Starbuck hadn't been informed of the exchange. He was not tied up or even guarded. I sent Rogue the thought that we better see what Kyle was up to, and we slipped and slid down a narrow hillside path to the trail, arriving just in front of the caravan.

Kyle was annoyed when he saw me in front of him. He could tell from my look that I knew something and was about to confront him with it.

"What's wrong with you?" he growled.

I told him.

"We can't do it. Even mother says so."

"You always pretend you've been talking to mother when you want to question my judgment."

I wanted to kick, scream, and hit.

"You make me so angry, Kyle, I'd like to strangle you."

"Try it, sister."

"Kyle, this is no time for a childish quarrel among siblings. I'm telling you that this exchange is not even logical. Megan doesn't want it, it's not even sensible. You can't trust the tincans."

"This time I can. I have something they want desperately. They'll make the trade."

"But, Kyle—"

"What's wrong with you, Miri? Don't you want mother back?"

I could hold back my tears no longer.

"Yes, of course I do."

"And aren't you willing to do anything to get her back?"

"Of—of course—course I am. But we shouldn't—"

"There is nothing to discuss, Miri. We trade Starbuck to the tincans for mother. Tonight. It is all arranged."

I looked back toward Starbuck, who could hear none

of what we had said. If I went to him and told him now, I'd be a traitor. If I became a traitor, it might mean that Megan would die, that my selfish sense of, what would you call it, ethics or honor or whatever had killed her.

I did not know what to do, and I could not stop crying.

I rode on, beside Kyle, Kyle keeping a watchful eye on me to make sure I was not urged toward betrayal. I tried to think of some solution. Tried desperately to think of something.

CHAPTER TWELVE

Occasionally Starbuck perversely wished the *Galactica* rescue team would be delayed. He had not had this much fun in ages. Miri's treatments had raised his spirits as well as cured his leg. New energy surged through veins, his muscles were revived, and his mind was clearer and less troubled than before. This damp, frequently grotesque planet, Antila, was better for him than any of those beautified and stylized therapy room fantasies.

He could swear that many of his good feelings emanated from Magician. They actually seemed to flow into him, a strong surge of, well, power from this bizarre black unicorn. Magician was some fine animal. Nothing like those stolid beasts of his therapy room adventures. Unlike the smooth coats of those fantasy creatures, Magician's was rough, with long bristly hairs. Still, one felt compelled to stroke at it regularly anyway, to continue patting Magician's neck, encouraging him, letting him know your confidence in him. Starbuck's hand might wind up raw and blistered, but the persistent surges of good feeling made it all worthwhile.

It was difficult to figure just how this telepathic connection with Magician functioned, but Starbuck had arrived at some conclusions about the temperamental unicorn. Magician, though clearly a sentient, even highly intelligent being, was not somebody you'd take to a party and expect to mingle. He had a quick temper, an independence fierce enough to scare off bullies and a willingness to pursue a goal beyond its limits. He was also ready, even eager, to take risks, to bluff, to twist any restriction or rule to his own favor. All of this knowledge about the animal came to Starbuck intuitively, in waves, in blocks, in lightning flashes, but rarely in understandable words, coherent language, clear sentences. He just seemed to absorb the information as if it just settled like snow (and sometimes driving rain) into his mind, injected itself into his vascular system, invaded his emotions. The only clear rationally-expressed 'thought' that seemed to come from Magician was, "Human, we are alike, you and I." Starbuck assumed that the similarity, whether the thought itself actually originated from the animal or merely emerged from his own subconscious, was the reason that the previously-aloof unicorn had chosen Starbuck as a rider. He also assumed that any change in that attitude would result in Starbuck being abruptly launched into the air and thrown through the trees by this massively well-muscled beast.

So engrossed was he in his theories about Magician, he nearly did not see Miri ride up to Kyle, who rather aggressively and pointedly had taken up the leadership position on the trail. That was all right with Starbuck. Kyle knew the terrain, he *should* ride point.

The brother and sister had a rather animated and angry discussion, but their whispered and urgent words did not carry to Starbuck. Miri frequently looked Starbuck's way, her lovely eyes troubled. Kyle appeared to declare an end to their dispute and they rode on together. Again Kyle edged his mount forward, as if to show his sister that his place was at the front of his troops.

Eventually they reached a clearing beside a river and Kyle held up his hand to halt the line of riders. The children on unicorns immediately dismounted. They briskly began opening packs and setting up a camp. Mysteriously, other children appeared from out of the forest and joined the main troops. These others must have been keeping pace with the riders all the way, or arriving at this chosen destination by their own special routes. Starbuck recognized Ratzi, who of course immediately began supervising food preparation. The Genie, her fingers working as deftly as they did on her magic tricks, manipulated the guy ropes of a tent. Laughing Jake gave the other children orders without saying a word, communicating through looks and gestures. Melysa, a shy sweet child who always had a book sticking out of a corner of her back pack, started a group of children on assembling a raft from logs and leather thongs. Starbuck wondered briefly why they were building a raft. For that matter, all the activity around this temporary camp indicated a prearranged scheme, one they were concealing from Starbuck for a purpose. Kyle had said only that they were setting out on a ride to show Starbuck some of the terrain. All this busy work suggested something beyond a tourist trip. As if to verify Starbuck's suspicion, Kyle drew out his horn and blew a trio of short blasts on it. In the distance a watchtower bell responded.

Starbuck rode to him.

"Look," he said, "I don't like to interfere with your setup here, but what you trying to do with those horn blasts? They can be heard from here to forever. Why go to all this trouble and preparation if you're going to give away our position?"

Kyle regarded Starbuck with a cool disdain.

"I am sending a challenge. It is our way. You do not understand. We shall move again soon anyway."

"Move again? You're pounding in tent poles! And what's the point of this challenge? I thought you were just showing me around the countryside. You didn't say anything about inviting a guest list of Cylons."

Anger rushed into Kyle's eyes. His voice sounded quite adolescent when he responded:

"Do not tell me how to command!"

In frustration Starbuck raised his hands. There was no talking to Kyle. He took everything as a challenge to his authority over this kiddie band of his. Miri, attracted by the anger in Kyle's voice, rode up, her eyes concerned.

Magician seemed to be transmitting a feeling of calmness, telling Starbuck to leave Kyle be. It was perhaps unfortunate that Starbuck had not yet learned to take advice from a unicorn.

"You're grandstanding, Kyle. There's no time for that in this—"

"Because you wear a starfleet uniform and fly a fighter, you think you should be in command here."

The petulance in Kyle's voice had an odd calming effect on Starbuck. Everything was now so evident. He should have seen that Kyle was afraid of him, should have seen that Kyle saw him as a threat to his role as leader. What the hell did Starbuck care about leadership of a troop of children? He was a warrior and he did warrior jobs, but he never cared who was in charge. Leaders didn't matter that much to him. He usually did pretty much what he wanted to do anyway.

"So that's it," he said to Kyle. "You're afraid I want to take over from you?"

Kyle glanced quickly away, his stare concentrated on the forest.

"I fear no such thing."

"Kyle, you know what he says is true," Miri said.

Kyle's shoulders tensed and he whirled Demon around to face her.

"I should've known. Should've known you'd side with anyone who's against me. Especially a starfleet warrior! He smiles at you and you choose him. Him over me, over mother!"

"Mother?" Starbuck asked. "You said your mother had been killed. That's not true, is it?"

Kyle and Miri stared at each other for a long time.

"You have to tell him, Kyle."

"I don't have to do anything. Not anything *you* say." She turned to Starbuck.

"He wants to exchange you for mother. Tonight."

"Miri—"

"Never mind, Kyle. I told you what mother said. You

wouldn't listen. Starbuck has to know."

Kyle made a gesture and Starbuck found himself surrounded by members of the band. They held weapons, Cylon rifles, spikes and swords. Kyle held a rifle and was sighting carefully down the barrel. It was all so pathetic, so childish.

"Kyle, it won't work," he said. "These are Cylons you're talking about. They'll never make a fair trade. You can't trust them."

Suddenly Kyle's coolness, his posture of leadership, disintegrated.

"We must have mother back," he said, his voice clouded by tears. "We must. I have to take this chance. For her. What do I care about you? A hotshot, a pilot pig, fallen to earth and trying to take over where he's not wanted. When have you sky-screamers from the *Galactica* or from anywhere in the twelve worlds ever cared about us on Antilla? Where was your fleet when we transmitted signals for help? Where were your precious warriors, *Lieutenant* Starbuck?"

"I'm afraid we were in a little mess of our own. A mess created by Cylon treachery, incidentally. If you agree to any sort of pact with them, it'll be just like the peace offer they made the starfleet, a peace offer that was merely a cover for an ambush of all our worlds."

"I don't wish to hear any more." Kyle turned to the strongest children, Laughing Jake and Herbert the Singer. "Bind him," he ordered.

"Kyle," Miri shouted, "I don't think—"

"That's an order!"

Starbuck knew there was no point in resistance. As Herbert the Singer and Laughing Jake lifted Starbuck off Magician, the unicorn reared and pushed at the two large children. He lunged between them, propelling Starbuck toward the nearby forest. Kyle raised his gun and aimed it at Magician's head.

"No, Kyle!" Miri shouted.

Magician gave a sidelong look at Miri. Rearing again,

he shoved Kyle to the ground. Starbuck found himself shouting, "Get away, get going, you can't help me now." There was understanding in Magician's dark eyes as he looked toward Starbuck and suddenly, in a magnificent leap, galloped into the forest. He was out of sight before Kyle, after rolling around clownishly on the ground, could retrieve his rifle and fire.

"Kyle, if you'd killed Magician, I'd have—"

"Shut up, Miri." He shouted to Laughing Jake and Herbert the Singer, "Tie Starbuck to a tree."

As Starbuck passed Miri, cooperating with his two captors, Miri leaned down toward him and whispered:

"I'm sorry. I could have—"

"Shush, Miri, I understand. This trade may make some sense after all, if you can trust your enemy. I just doubt it."

"I, also."

Starbuck sighed.

"Well, if you can get your mother back, it might be worth it. And don't forget, as Kyle says, I'm a starfleet warrior. I'm supposed to take care of myself. I'll find a way."

"I wish I could believe you."

"So do I."

Miri's eyes were tearful. Starbuck could not look at her any more. He allowed himself to be taken to the tree, where Laughing Jake and Herbert the Singer, their fingers working deftly, bound him in astonishingly tight knots.

CHAPTER THIRTEEN

Lucifer's spirits might have risen a bit if he had known that Starbuck was the Galactican pilot who had crashed on Antila. He remembered Starbuck well, even a bit fondly—at least as fondly as an ambulatory sentient computer was capable of. It was, after all, not long ago that Starbuck had been a prisoner on the Cylon base star. The brash young lieutenant, at ease among his enemies, taught Lucifer a popular human card game called pyramid. Pyramid was basically a game of melding, of forming unique combinations, and—above all—of bluffing. Clever, even illogical, bluffing. Starbuck said that, for most pyramid players skill was the most important factor, except for the few who had been blessed with the uniquely human ability that ranked above skill, an ability they called luck. Starbuck was one of the lucky ones, at least he claimed that, and he proved it more than once to Lucifer in their sessions of playing pyramid. Lucifer had filed the precise details of all of these games in his memory banks and occasionally he reviewed them. Now he thought he had figured out a system that would counter Starbuck's luck. All Lucifer needed was the reappearance of Starbuck so he could test out his theories on him. He would have easily convinced himself to alter course for Antila if it meant that he could snatch Starbuck for some rousing games of pyramid.

Once he had suggested to Baltar that the two of them could engage in a round of pyramid. Baltar had sneered and said that games were for the unrational being. Lucifer had argued that, since logic played its part in pyramid, a large amount of rationality did go into the game. Baltar, sneering further, said that the rationality of such games was an empty one, futile moves toward a meaningless goal. Games were for children, Baltar said, then added with one of his characteristically insulting chuckles that of course since Lucifer was a comparatively recent cybernetic advancement perhaps he could be considered a child. Lucifer decided Baltar didn't deserve a response and glided rapidly out of the man's sight.

It was now time for conference. Each duty-tour Baltar insisted that he and Lucifer get together to discuss matters, even the most trivial events. Baltar, like most humans, was fascinated with trivial details. Conferences were a habit that the human had acquired from years of serving on subcommittees, then committees, then rising to the position of full-fledged member of the ruling body, the Council of Twelve. He seemed to need regular meetings, or else he became quite edgy.

Lucifer glided into the command room. Baltar lounged in the communications console chair, swinging it slightly from side to side with the smooth regular motions of a man at peace with himself.

"Still no word from Antila?" Lucifer asked.

"You are becoming obsessive about Antila, Lucifer. One might say that you could use a few sessions of what we humans call therapy."

"Therapy?"

"A bit of analysis of your thinking and feelings— though I know that feelings are meaningless to you, even if you do have them. A bit of help to aid you in adjusting to your troubles, your problems, your irrational leanings."

"I have neither troubles, problems, nor irrational leanings."

Actually, he thought, he did, though he would never admit them. Baltar was simultaneously a trouble, a problem, and Lucifer was aware of frequent *irrational leanings* in Baltar's direction.

"You needn't get in a snit," Baltar said. "Spectre will

contact us when he has something to report."

"It has been a long time since his last communication. He should have something by now. Perhaps he feels his information will not be received satisfactorily by you, Baltar."

Baltar looked quizzically at Lucifer.

"Hmmm. You've got something odd going on in that light bulb of a head, Lucifer. What are you implying?"

Lucifer hated it when Baltar called his head a light bulb. Cylons, masters of indirect lighting sources, did not have such primitive devices as light bulbs. Humans did, and their shape was nothing like Lucifer's head. Well, not much anyway.

"It has come to my attention," Lucifer said, "that Spectre is a master at requisitioning materials. He has supplies on Antila that no garrison that size would require except in the most extreme situations. He has managed, for example, to acquire more fuel than any other garrison in the sector, and his is the smallest garrison in the sector."

Baltar smiled.

"If you think you're distressing me, you're mistaken. I'm even more impressed with our Spectre. Obviously, he's an efficient stockpiler, a marvelous trait in a garrison commander."

"But he also keeps ordering weapons, laser rifles and metron bombs."

"So?"

"He *alleges* that the colony on Antila was completely destroyed. He has no reason for that much weaponry to defend what is essentially an out-of-the-way outpost."

Baltar cleared his throat and studied his stubby-fingered hands.

"I'm surprised at you, Lucifer. Amassing circumstantial evidence to cruelly demean the work of an efficient fellow officer."

"It is important that—"

"I do understand what you are saying, Lucifer. You

mean to imply that, if his records are of such a questionable nature, that he is also capable of submitting false reports to us."

"Speaking from past experience, I would say it is not beyond his programming."

Baltar laughed, his laughter creating a resounding echo in the cavernous command room.

"Lucifer! I do believe you are jealous."

"That is not part of my programming."

In fact, though, it was. Lying was also a part of his programming. Deception had become vital since he had been forced to deal with Baltar on a regular basis.

"If Spectre is as efficient as you say," Lucifer said, "then we should have much more information about the captured Galactican pilot by now."

Baltar shrugged.

"That perhaps shows Spectre's meticulous efficiency. He is not ready to report prematurely anything that— wait, a signal is coming in now. From *Antila*, Lucifer. I am not surprised."

Lucifer suppressed saying that *he* was.

"Commander Spectre reporting, sir," said the image of Spectre as it formed on the screen from dots into a reasonable facsimile of the individual.

"Ah, Spectre," Baltar said. "We have just been . . . discussing your abilities. Do you now have the present coordinates of the *Galactica*?"

Spectre hesitated a beat.

"Well, not exactly, sir."

"Hmmm," Lucifer muttered softly. Baltar, clearly annoyed, glared at him.

"Go on, Spectre," Baltar said.

"I'm afraid the colonial warrior was seriously injured in the crash. We are attempting to repair his body in order to extract the information you require."

Repair? Lucifer thought. Spectre talked of this pilot's injury as if were merely circuitry to be worked on and reconnected. Humans were not as easily fixed as computers or robots, after all.

"I see," Baltar said. "How long do you estimate that this . . . this repair process will take?"

"Not long. As soon as we can improve him physically, he should respond to torture."

That seemed peculiar to Lucifer. First you 'repair' the man, then you wreck him again. Sometimes he wondered if information was worth the trouble one went to in order to get it.

"I'm not concerned with the fate of the colonial warrior, Spectre," Baltar said. "But I'm counting on you to get the information about the *Galactica*. Our cat-and-mouse game with that battlestar has just about ended, I feel."

"I understand your needs, sir, and let me say that it is a distinct honor to serve the illustrious Count Baltar."

"I am impressed that you know my human title."

"Sir, you are a legend to us."

"Oh, my," Lucifer muttered. He had not realized that the earlier series had ever been programmed for such obvious and overmannered obsequiousness. Obvious or not, it worked. Baltar was smiling smugly as he said:

"Well, thank you, Spectre."

"I will report again soon, sir."

"By all means."

"By your command."

Baltar nodded and Spectre's image faded from the screen.

"You see, Lucifer," Baltar said, turning away from the console, "Spectre has provided us with logical explanations."

"Yes, I see," Lucifer said. His doubts must have somehow communicated themselves to Baltar, for the human commented:

"Lucifer, you'd be surprised to find out that this jealousy between classes of computers is nothing compared to that among classes of humankind."

This observation caused Baltar, irrationally, to laugh uproariously.

As Spectre switched off his transmitter, Hilltop appeared beside him, as usual.

"If I may say so, honored sir, I had not realized that such deceptions were possible within the chain of command."

"Oh, they are, Hilltop, they are. In some ways, they are what keep the links in the chain solid."

Hilltop seemed ready to express further doubt, but Spectre waved him away. He was feeling pretty proud of himself, proud of the way he was turning an untenable situation to his advantage, proud of the way he was clearly impressing Baltar. There *was* a place for him in the Cylon chain of command, he was positive, and its position could be considerably higher than commander of a tiny garrison on an out-of-the-way, edge-of-the-universe, bleak, ugly, miserable, damp, beyond all rationality planet.

CHAPTER FOURTEEN

FROM MIRI'S BOOK:
Kyle set several of the children to work binding together
the raft. I could sense his eyes on me as I checked
Starbuck's injured leg. The gash had just about healed,
as I had expected, but I decided to keep the leg bandaged
and so rewrapped the green-blue leaves around the poultice.

"You needn't worry about an infection," I said to my
patient. "I applied the horn-paste in time. Your leg looks
almost healed."

"Terrific," Starbuck muttered. "I can walk with digni-
ty to my execution."

I wanted to reach out and hold him to me, but Kyle
would interfere if I showed Starbuck any affection. Anyway, I knew he feared I might untie the lieutenant and,
to tell the truth, if I could have figured out a way to untie
him quickly, before Kyle could respond, I would have
done it. But the knots had been made by Herbert the
Singer and Laughing Jake. They were thick and secure.

"Actually," Starbuck continued, "Cylons aren't exactly quick to execute. They like to see what little pains
they can inflict on—"

"Please, don't," I said. "Perhaps they won't . . ."

"Kill me? Miri, you lived through their invasion,
you've been spying on them long enough. You know
what they do to people."

"They haven't executed mother or the other prisoners."

Starbuck sighed. I felt like a child and briefly resented
him for making me feel that way.

"Maybe not," he said. "But, if that's so, they're saving their lives for a reason. To get information, to research the capacity of the human being for pain, to—to make just such an exchange as this. Don't make the mistake of thinking they see us the way we see each other. We're just objects to them, and it doesn't much matter whether they kill us or experiment on our bodies."

"Perhaps we can attack them and get you back. Or maybe we can trade again for you, or—"

"How? By trading another human for me? No thanks. I couldn't live with that."

"That's what mother said about this trade. I was supposed to stop it. But Kyle wouldn't listen. I don't know how to help, I just don't . . ."

"Keep talking."

"Why?"

"Just keep talking."

Gradually I perceived what was happening. Magician, blending in with the forest's darkness, had returned. He was standing just behind Starbuck. I don't know how Starbuck knew that. He had not even glanced back in the direction of the forest. He must have picked up a thought from Magician. I started talking rapidly about mother.

"Megan says we have no right to trade in human beings. Another prisoner argued with her."

Magician leaned his head down, his horn pointing toward Starbuck's bound wrists.

"Keep talking, Miri."

"I don't—I can't think of—there's this picture in this storeroom. It's a unicorn. A woman on it. It's beautiful. I don't know how to describe it."

Magician worked at the knots on Starbuck's wrists, the sharp tip of his horn slipping into the first knot-loop and laboriously loosening it until, with a jerk of his head, he had untied it. Shaking his head, he started working on the next loop and unknotted it faster. I babbled on about the picture, not even sure of what I was saying.

I nearly shrieked as Magician freed the last strands of rope from Starbuck's wrists.

Starbuck kept his wrists together but began to work his way sideways around the tree. He slowly brought his legs under him in a crouch, ready to stand and spring onto Magician's back.

Suddenly Kyle screamed with rage.

The other children, alerted, raced to us. Starbuck started to make a leap toward Magician, but Laughing Jake managed to get in his way, and successfully block him. Starbuck nudged Jake a bit, but the other children were all over him, pushing him to the ground, holding him down, pygmies using their weight collectively to keep the giant from moving. Magician tried to interfere and pushed at Jake, who wisely let himself be edged forward.

Kyle shot his rifle. Its beam came close to Magician's head. Magician whirled and immediately vanished into the black forest. I almost grabbed Jake's pistol from its holster to shoot Kyle. That time I think Kyle really *had* meant to kill Magician.

Kyle told Jake and Herbert not to bother with retying Starbuck to the tree. He had them replace the younger children in holding Starbuck down on the ground, then he strode to the river bank, checked the raft by pulling at its leather bindings, then setting it afloat to see how it set in the water. Satisfied, he returned.

"The raft is ready. It will soon be time."

"The trade won't work, Kyle," Starbuck said, his voice a little breathless since Jake was sitting on his chest.

"You underestimate me, pilot. That's been your problem all along. It's why I was able to trick you. I've planned this trade rather well. The tincans will put mother in a boat and launch her toward us. We will simultaneously launch you toward them. Neither side can take advantage of the other, you see that?"

"I'll take all the action and any side bets you want

to make that there's a catch in this somewhere."

"Kyle," I said, "he's right. It's what mother said about this being a mistake."

"You shut up about mother. We need her back."

"*You* do."

"And you don't, I suppose. You've gotten hard, sister."

"Of course I want her back, but this is not the way."

Kyle's eyes became icy.

"It is a necessary tactical move," he said.

"Necessary? Tactical? You've gone out of your head with all this military garbage. We're talking about human beings here, not tactics. We're talking about trading Starbuck—"

"For our mother! Miri, I know what I'm doing." A whine had come into his voice. "Haven't I led well since the invasion?"

"Yes, but we are not an army! Look around you. These are not warriors. They're just children. Go on, look."

For a moment my words got to him. He glanced toward the stream where the younger children were anchoring the raft, some of their movements in the water playful. He looked over at the older children, who held their various weapons ready. He looked back at Jake and Herbert holding Starbuck down on the ground.

"Yes. Children. That's why we need Megan back, to—"

"Kyle," Starbuck said. "This might surprise you, but I do agree with you. I can see that you all do need Megan, plus any of the other parents of these children who are still alive. But—"

"Kyle! Miri! Children!" interrupted the voice of Megan from across the river. The tincans had lit a small fire and brought her next to it, so we could see her. She was dressed in a fresh blue blouse, creased darker blue slacks, shiny black boots. There was a bright yellow scarf around her head, undoubtedly chosen by Spectre to hide her thinning hair from us.

"Mother!" I cried. I could not help it.

The other children cheered. Kyle looked prouder than ever. He stared down at Starbuck and said:

"I'm sorry, but this is my choice."

"If you'll just listen to me . . ."

"There's no point in listening. I won't hear a word you say, lieutenant."

Surprisingly, there was pain in Kyle's face as he turned away from Starbuck. He hadn't always been like this, and I think he knew it wasn't in his nature. Still, he was a strong commander—maybe too strong—and never avoided a hard decision. He raised his horn and blew three short blasts.

The signal to exchange.

I wanted to run, follow Magician into the darkness of the forest, lose myself there, never come out. At the same time I wanted desperately for the boat to cross the river and hold Megan close to me again.

Heal her wounds.

Have her heal mine.

CHAPTER FIFTEEN

Megan cursed herself for calling the children's names first. She meant to say more, to shout to Kyle to give up this misguided idea, but a Cylon grabbed her by the arm, pulled her out of the firelight, and clamped a metal hand over her mouth.

She watched Spectre glide toward the fire and consult with a centurion. Across the river Kyle blew his horn three times.

"That's the signal," Spectre said. "We can commence the exchange."

He tilted his head toward Megan.

"Take the woman away!"

Away! Megan thought. She had been right all along. Spectre never had intended to go through with the exchange. He was tricking Kyle to obtain the colonial warrior. The miserable rust-box! Desperately she began searching for a way to warn the children, but, silencing her with his hand, the guard maneuvered her away. She could no longer see even the outlines of Kyle, Miri, or the other children across the river.

She was placed roughly against a tree, gagged, then forced to sit. Irrationally, she noticed how crisp and fresh her new garments felt, and she wondered if they would allow her to wear the clothes back in her cell. What did that matter, though? They would only become dirty and gray instantly.

Maybe they would kill her, execute her and the cap-

tured pilot together. That might be all right. She would
not mind dying in fresh clothes.

Spectre's voice was mechanically professorial as he
instructed his aide on the art of being devious.

"You will observe, Hilltop, that we have removed the
prisoner Megan from the immediate area."

"Yes, honored sir. I did notice that."

"Good. Now, what do you suppose we are going to
do about the exchange?"

Hilltop did not say anything for a moment. A couple
of tricky whirring sounds, emanating from somewhere
inside his aide, disturbed Spectre. Whirs were not good
and were often a prelude to major circuitry dysfunction.

"Do we default, sir, then attack the enemy in a wide-
spread assault?"

Spectre liked Hilltop's response. It showed the aide
could at least think strategically.

"No, Hilltop, but not bad. While you were busy earlier, assembling the patrol, I did my own bit of assembling. I made a copy of Megan in my laboratory."

At a gesture from Spectre, a centurion unwrapped
what was essentially a doll-version of Megan, life-size.
For a hasty makeshift rendering, the likeness was remarkably accurate. It was indeed, Spectre thought, a
craftsmanlike job. The expression on its plastic face was
gaunt and disturbed. Its clothing duplicated the new garments given the real Megan to wear for the occasion.

"A very impressive duplication, honored sir," Hilltop
said. "I had not realized such a model was possible."

Spectre leaned toward Hilltop. A strain of amusement
came into his voice.

"I can build anything, Hilltop. I am an expert at cybernetic mechanics. Don't forget, I built you, Hilltop."

"Oh yes, sir. I would assume that, however, this copy
is not, like me, animate."

"Quite right, although, to be technical, you are not
exactly animate either. However, I did not need to give

the doll circuits for thinking or speaking. It is just a shell, merely a hollow replication."

"I am continually impressed, sir, by the methods with which you utilize our supplies of materials to accomplish the most astonishing effects."

Spectre stared a long time at Hilltop, the red lights of his eyes almost at a standstill.

"Hmmm," he said, "I don't recall programming flattery into your model."

"I am quite sincere, sir."

"You must be. Yes, you must be. Well, place the replication in the boat and launch it."

"Yes, sir."

Mist had collected quickly on the surface of the dark river. Wisps of it rose like gray flames. The centurions lifted the replication of Megan onto the boat and, at Spectre's command, pushed it into the water. It floated slowly toward the opposite shore.

"We have kept our part of the bargain," Spectre shouted to the children. "Our boat is heading your way. Now, where is the colonial warrior?"

There was a short pause, a loud splash, and a call from Kyle:

"The bargain is complete. Here is your pilot, tincan!"

In the misty darkness, the passing of the two craft was barely visible. Spectre was pleased to see the bent-shouldered outline of the starfleet pilot tied to a raft. He was already planning his next transmission to Baltar. This time Lucifer would squirm. That is, if he had been programmed for that response.

CHAPTER SIXTEEN

FROM MIRI'S BOOK:
We had not seen Megan since her too-brief appearance in the firelight. The children grew steadily restless, milled about on the river bank like predators without prey. The dark night was like a blanket thrown hastily over us, to smother us or to shield us from truth. After Kyle blew the signal on his horn, all we could hear from the other side of the river were the usual mysterious Cylon clanking sounds.

Kyle raised his left hand, a signal for Laughing Jake and Herbert the Singer to bring our captive forward. My own eyes on the verge of tears, I stared into Starbuck's eyes. They were cool, resigned. He showed no fright, no grimness, not even any anger at us for deceiving him and using him as a pawn in a power game. And he must have seen the power game as precisely that: a children's game played with plastic pieces on a cardboard slab. If I had had the strength, I might have grabbed Starbuck away from his guards, and run with him into the forest. He was clever, he was a warrior, he knew strategy, he could have devised a plan to rescue mother without this kind of human sacrifice. And I realized suddenly that was what this act was. A human sacrifice. An offering of a life to our invader-gods in order to have our prayer answered. In so short a time we had reverted to this primitive state. We had come to Antila as a group of worldly-wise intellectual rebels with firm ideas for sensible progress, and we had regressed to a shabby outlaw band of children eager to sacrifice a man. We might as well have thrown him alive onto a burning pyre and danced to evil gods.

Finally the return signal came. The wretched voice of Spectre came to us from across the river. I could have sworn that the dampness of the air added an undertone of static to its already wavery sound. He announced that he was launching the boat holding mother. Kyle answered that we were keeping our part of the bargain, and he gestured to Jake and Herbert to place Starbuck onto our makeshift raft. Starbuck stepped onto the raft without a pause, confidently, as if he were in complete control of the situation. Ratzi appeared suddenly from behind Jake's large body and took a couple of steps toward the raft. She seemed determined to accompany Starbuck on the crossing, but Kyle, seizing her by the shoulders, held her back. The Genie idly shuffled a pack of cards. I suddenly realized that they were Starbuck's cards. I'd seen them earlier in his flight-jacket shoulder pocket. Jergin stood by our fire and made odd gestures in the light of the flames, a delicate dance with her hands, her thin flexible fingers. The twins, Nilz and Robus, held each other, managing to look hopeful and terrified simultaneously.

Quickly Jake and Herbert secured Starbuck to the raft and, at Kyle's command, pushed it outward. The mists rising from the water looked to me like bars already imprisoning Starbuck. He did not look back. He became a shape, a dark outline, drifting away from us. In the middle of the river, another dark outline appeared and, for a moment, it looked as if the two boats might collide, link up and start on a new course downstream together. After they had passed, Starbuck called back:

"Miri! Your mother was right. They've—"

But the rest of what he said was lost as the tincans started making strange noises among themselves, talking together as if commanded to. Nilz, Robus, and Ariadne waded out into the water, shouting:

"It's mother. It's mother."

Kyle sent me a very haughty look. For the moment, he was inordinately proud of himself. I ignored him, and stared out at the river. First I saw that the clothes on the raft figure were the same new garments I had seen on Megan in the firelight. Then I recognized Megan's face. I thought it was Megan's face. Yet there was an emptiness in it. A blank stare, an unmoving mouth. Oh my god, I thought, they've killed her first. That's the catch in their deal. They'd sent us mother, but killed her first. I looked at Kyle. Some of the pride had left his eyes. He seemed to be seeing the same thing I was. This was our mother and she looked lifeless. I wanted to scream. So, I suspect, did Kyle.

Kyle rushed out to the water, his legs churning up gigantic splashes. He joined Nilz, Robus, and Ariadne, and all four of them pulled strenuously at the raft, brought it shoreward. Kyle splashed around to the rear of the boat, and with a powerful shove, pushed it up on land.

"Mother," I cried, "we're—"

Then I saw the truth. It was not Megan, it was not even the corpse of Megan. It was a duplicate, a replication, a clever reproduction of our mother meant to fool us. Starbuck was right. Megan was right. I was right. Spectre had had no intention of keeping Kyle's bargain. This was the Cylon style of trade—one living human being for a mockup copy. It was like the fake peace offer Starbuck had described to me, when the Cylons had tempted the human side with peace while they were actually setting up the immense destruction of not only the fleet but all of the twelve home worlds.

"Oh, Kyle," I said. He looked stunned. He looked like a child who had just been cheated in a war game, whose pieces had just been knocked off the table by his opponent. He looked ready to cry. My words to him, which were intended sympathetically, were taken by him as a rebuke.

"Don't speak to me, sister," he muttered. "Don't speak to me."

I wanted to hold him, soothe him with words or a song, minister to his sorrow. But I, the healer, could do nothing. I merely stood there, did what he said. I didn't speak to him.

Then a thought forced its way into my head—not a thought really, more a feeling. Don't despair. Then the thought became clearer, formed into words. The man is just reaching the other side. He is not yet in the enemy prison. It will take them time to move. I can save him.

Then I realized where the thought was coming from. Magician.

He was back there in the darkness, calling to me.

The thoughts stopped. I knew he had gone to help. I would follow, help him if I could.

Edging backwards silently, I summoned Rogue, told him to wait for me at the edge of the forest. Mounting him quickly, I urged him into the forest. As we cleared the border of trees, I sneaked one look back. Kyle was standing as before, staring at the replication of Megan. Suddenly he knelt down and picked it up, held it to him, began to cry. That's the last I saw of him as the darkness of the forest enveloped me.

CHAPTER SEVENTEEN

Even through the thick mist, Starbuck could see that the figure on the other raft was not real. He tried to shout the truth back to Miri, but a sudden, obviously calculated, burst of noise from the Cylon riverside drowned him out. He strained at his bonds but the two strong boys had tied him up too efficiently. He was not only tightly bound, but he was also secured to the raft so he could not tip it over.

All he could do was float serenely toward the opposite bank. The shapes standing there became gradually distinct. First he saw a pair of red lights directed right at him, but these lights did not belong to a typical Cylon. This one was bulb-headed, phantomlike. In fact, he resembled Lucifer, the walking computer Starbuck had encountered, and rather liked, aboard Baltar's base ship. This one was clearly a more primitive model, not fitted out with all the googaws and flimflam that had adorned Lucifer. Other Cylons gathered around this figure, apparently awaiting his orders. Could he be their leader? Their deference certainly suggested that.

They allowed the raft to hit the bank before even reaching for Starbuck. They were oddly delicate about shoring the raft, as if they did not care to pollute themselves with swamp water. He had never known Cylons to be so fussy before. This group, in fact, did not even move like Cylons he had seen. If anything, their movements were more graceful, more supple, than the normal Cylon. Still clumsy, but with more style to their awkwardness.

As soon as they had freed him from the raft, keeping

119

his hands tied behind him, they forced him to stand up and step to shore. They pushed him toward their leader, who glided up to Starbuck in much the same manner Lucifer had so long ago. The leader made a signal for the guards to halt, then said to the prisoner:

"My humblest greetings to you, sir. I have not before met a colonial warrior personally."

"The pleasure's mine, I'm sure."

"You are quite gracious."

"I am quite sarcastic."

"I do appreciate sarcasm and irony. Delightful human traits, in truth. My name is Spectre." Spectre waited for Starbuck to respond, but instead the human focussed on the leader's moving eyes. "And your name, pilot?"

"You'll have to work for that, cap."

"But you're from the *Galactica*. I can see that from your insignia."

"This shopworn patch? I won it in a card game. Really I'm from a tramp freighter called *The Floating Dustbin*."

"I enjoy human jokes, too, even when they are difficult to understand."

"Good. I can drag out my worst material for you."

"Please do. Take him away, centurions."

His guards hit his shoulders roughly and he was again shoved forward, away from the river. From the other side of the water, he heard disappointed groans. The children must have just then realized that the Megan delivered on the Cylon boat was a fake. Poor kids, they'd learned an important lesson in deceit. Too bad it was going to cost Starbuck his life.

His guards led him to Megan, who sat dazedly beneath a tree. She looked up at Starbuck with blank eyes. Her mouth was covered by a gag. A centurion forced her to stand, then removed the gag. She could hardly walk, and Starbuck put his arm around her to hold her up. She was thin, light. The weightlessness of her body went appropriately with the gaunt look of her face. Still, one could see the prettiness of Miri in Megan, in spite of her prison pallor and the ravages of illness. Megan seemed to want to talk desperately, but her mouth would not work.

"Don't you guys have any vehicles?" Starbuck said to the nearest guard. "A wagon, for God's sake? This woman's been through enough, she doesn't have to be forced to walk like—"

"Quiet, pilot," the guard said. "There will be a land transport when we reach the road."

"Thanks for trying," Megan whispered, her voice scratchy and weak. "But I can make it."

"You sure?"

"They've been pushing me around for some time now. I'm still moving on my own, aren't I? Just barely, but moving."

"I can see where your daughter gets her courage."

Megan smiled. Her teeth were yellowed and coated. She tried to say more, but again her voice failed her.

They reached the land transport, a crude three-wheeled contraption that pulled a rickety small cart. Starbuck and Megan were pushed to the floor of the cart, onto a thin layer of straw.

"They believe in elegance, I see," Starbuck said.

Megan nodded.

"Only the best," she managed to whisper.

She lay back and immediately fell asleep. She was so thin, Starbuck thought. She appeared ready to waste away at any moment. No wonder there was such urgency on the part of Kyle to save her. He must have sensed that they had to rescue her soon.

She came awake suddenly, after they had ridden quite a distance. Her eyes were less yellow in the corners, and a spot of color had appeared in each cheek. The color was not the proper red of healthiness, but at least it was color.

"I feel better," she said, her voice stronger. "I have periods of health, it seems. I'm sorry, warrior, that you were caught in this trap. Kyle meant well, but—"

"It's all right. My name is Starbuck, Megan. You needn't call me warrior."

"I'll try not to. But, in a way, you're my enemy just as much as Spectre and his Cylons. We fled Scorpia in the first place because of warlike humans."

"I assure you I'm not warlike, not in the way you mean. I fight the battles, but that's not the same as being warlike."

"Oh?"

"Believe me, I have no love for war. Where I come from we're all sick of war; maybe the warriors even more than the rest. We've been fighting all our lives. The art of war has no attraction for us. It's not an art, in fact, its a job and a pretty miserable, but highly necessary one at that."

"Where do you come from?"

"The Battlestar *Galactica*."

"Ah, I've heard of that ship. It had a great reputation, according to what news got through to our colony of the war. Its commander is much admired, I believe."

"Yes. Commander Adama. He still speaks of peace with a gleam in his eye. He expects to find it in a place called Earth."

Megan appeared impressed. She leaned closer to Starbuck.

"I thought Earth was just a legend."

"Not to Adama. He claims he has proof. Some words he read on the wall of an ancient tomb before Cylon bombs destroyed it. I don't know what he read but, whatever it was, it's given him great faith that we'll find Earth, and I have faith in him."

"Such loyalty. Characteristic of the military spirit."

"You tend to slip into dogma rather easily, Megan."

"Forgive me. I didn't mean that it wasn't an admirable trait, only that it was characteristic. You were just talking of faith yourself. I suppose we each respond to our own dogma."

"I suppose."

Megan's eyes cleared for a moment, becoming youthful, less tired.

"You think we failed here on Antila, don't you?"

"I really don't know enough about it to—"

"Well, we did fail. But not because we were against war, not even because we were invaded by Cylons. The threat of evil coming from the outside was always real, always possible. But the work inside the colony was worthwhile and, even at its worst, productive. We were beginning to find our way back to the old ideas, the ones that had gotten us shipped off Scorpia in the first place. We can do it again. That's what colonies like ours are all about, really—striving, trying to get to a sense of something more than living out one's life in tedious quests. Or in war. You want to bite off my head, don't you?"

Megan could not tell what Starbuck was thinking, especially since he smiled through her attack on him.

"I'm not against you," he said. "I admire what you people tried to do here. It may surprise you to know that there's a part of me that'd probably enjoy living and working in a useful society like yours. A machine revealed that part of myself to me not long ago, in fact. But my programming's different, I guess."

"That's a pretty coldhearted way to put it, Starbuck. Programming. I mean, you're not a machine."

"No, I'm not. And yes I am. Yes, we all are. We're all presented with various programs at various times of our lives. Sometimes we accept them, sometimes we kick them back, sometimes we just go along without any conscious decision. Look, I was brought up in a less warlike society than Scorpia's. Caprica was—"

"They were *all* warlike, *all* the twelve worlds."

Starbuck shrugged.

"Maybe so. From your vantage point. But there were differences. If I had been born on Scorpia, perhaps I'd be the fiercest fighter in the fleet and not entertain occasional doubts, not wish for my peaceful home back on Caprica to be restored. But, see, my programming's for war, and I've accepted that. I'd like to get out some-time and get a better scam but—"

"But what?"

"I don't know. It's a . . . problem I haven't been able to resolve. Maybe I'll never resolve it."

"I was born on Scorpia and I didn't become a fierce fighter."

"Didn't you?"

Megan looked at him, puzzled, then got his point. She laughed.

"I suppose you're right. In my own way, I've fought pretty fierce battles here, even *before* the Cylons came. Maybe it's just a question of rechanneling resources."

"Or of reprogramming."

"Have it your way, *warrior*."

"See, you even use the word warrior as a weapon. Fierce. I think, if we can get you out of this jam, you can really make a go of your colony. At least if *you* take charge, Megan. You can do it. I can see that, feel that."

She smiled.

"Now you, the *warrior*, are encouraging me to return to my *peaceful* life."

"By all means. Do. Please do."

"Would you stay with us, help us to restore the col-ony?"

A wistful look clouded Starbuck's eyes.

"I wish I could. I really do. But I have to go on. On with my own quest, if you will."

"To rejoin your ship and search for this mythical Earth?"

He nodded.

"In a way, yeah. We've got to keep going, searching. We even have to keep fighting the Cylons. You only have a taste of their evil here. But I have a feeling. . . ."

"Yes?"

"I just can't see myself getting to Earth. Maybe others will make it, but I just think that a lot of us will merely

keep the quest going, while others—descendants perhaps—will be the discoverers, the—"

"Perhaps you're just depressed. A kind of battle fatigue. Or nonbattle fatigue. Stuck here, away from your
ship and all."

"Yeah, maybe."

They rode in silence for a long while. Behind them
the Cylon guards walked, their pace rapid even through
the treacherous terrain.

"They just don't look right," Starbuck said.

"What? I'm afraid I don't—"

"These Cylons. The outfits are right, the red lights
move right, but there's something different. They move
more easily, more—"

"That's Spectre's work."

"Their leader."

"Yes. He's a cybernetic expert, proficient at making
other models more or less in the same model series from
which he originates. He makes them less clever, of
course, and programs an absolute obedience into—"

"Wait," Starbuck interrupted, recalling the Cylon in
the forest that he had thought was just an abandoned
uniform. It had been so weightless. "You're saying that
some of these Cylons are not the real thing? That they're
not genuine aliens at all, but cybernetic devices?"

Megan nodded.

"I'm beginning to suspect that none of them are from
the original landing party," she said. "When they came,
Cylons were more susceptible to the wretched diseases
of this planet than ever our colony was. I can't be sure,
but I think they've all died off, and Spectre has built
these fake Cylon warriors to take their place."

"But why?"

"Can't be sure. Perhaps he realizes that reinforce-
ments would just contract the planet's diseases and die
just as quickly as the originals. Perhaps he prefers an
army over which he has absolute control without wor-
rying about his position being usurped by a real Cylon

who outranks him. He was not the first leader here, you know. Whatever the reason, they all serve the same purpose for him. He maintains his power, his position as commander is not threatened, and nobody transfers him away from a post where he enjoys the kind of power that a cybernetic creation rarely achieves. But all these are just suppositions. He doesn't choose to confide in me. Just never trust Spectre, that's all I can say for sure. He's worse than a killer soldier, he's a power-hungry bureaucrat."

"This place gets crazier all the—"

Starbuck was interrupted by a sudden movement among the marching Cylon guards, followed by a shout from Spectre who was sitting at the front of the three-wheeled vehicle pulling the wagon.

"What's wrong back there?"

As if in response, three Cylons fell to the ground. Bounding over them in a magnificent graceful leap was Magician, his black hide darker than the night itself.

While watching the unicorn's leap, Starbuck received a thought from him:

Swing onto my back as I race by the wagon!

"Get on your feet, Megan," Starbuck whispered.

"Why?"

"Never mind. Just get up!"

Magician had disappeared into the darkness on the opposite side of the road.

Another thought: I'm about to make my run now.

Wait for Megan, Starbuck returned. Take both of us.

No time. Save her later. Here I come!

Megan almost got to her feet then a lurch of the wagon sent her falling backward against the wagonside. Spectre shouted orders to his troops, telling the ones on the ground to get up, telling those still standing to prepare for another attack.

Magician appeared near the wagon. As soon as he saw the unicorn, Starbuck started his leap over the side. It was perfectly timed. He came down on Magician's back just as the animal passed the wagon. Starbuck nearly slid backward and off the unicorn, but managed to hold on for dear life.

"We'll be back for you, Megan!" Starbuck yelled as Magician bounded back into the forest's darkness. Starbuck heard the shrilly mechanical voice of Spectre fading as they galloped away.

We must go back, save Megan, he thought.

No.

Please.

Pause, then: All right, one try. Only one try.

Magician swung around without breaking pace and headed back toward the road, where the sounds of turmoil were just beginning to subside. Megan still clung to the side of the wagon, looking outward. As they halted near the edge of the trees, Starbuck thought:

She's very light, almost weightless. You stop next to her side of the wagon, I'll lift her out.

It won't work.

We'll try.

All right, the one try and the one try only.

Timing his jump perfectly, Magician was out on the road again, just behind the patrol. He raced right through the patrol, scattering Cylons left and right, most of them plunging to the ground.

"Megan!" Starbuck shouted. "Reach for me!"

She held out her thin arms as Magician came to an abrupt stop. Putting his arm around her shoulders, Starbuck half-lifted Megan out of the wagon. Spectre shouted an order to shoot.

"Use your feet, Megan, scramble over the side," Starbuck cried.

"I can't. I'm too weak. I—"

The Cylons started firing. A shot hit Megan immediately, and Starbuck felt her go limp in his arms. He almost lifted her all the way out, but her clothing had caught on a metal outcropping on the inside of the wagon.

Let her go, Magician thought. We can't stay like this. But I—

LET HER GO!

Starbuck released his hold, and Megan fell back unconscious into the wagon. Magician immediately started to gallop away, and they were quickly surrounded by darkness again, although this time the night was interrupted by lines of light from Cylon rifles.

They were out of range quickly.

Are you all right, Magician? Starbuck thought and, in response, he received waves of feeling from the animal, informing him that everything was okay except for a couple grazing wounds on his tough hide.

I may have killed her. I may have killed Megan just for a fool act of—

No, she's alive. I can sense her aliveness. She is hurt but she is alive.

Thank God. We must try again to rescue her, we must—

Not this time. One time only, that was my promise.

Promises are important to you.

They are everything.

There is something magical about you, Magician.

Starbuck received warm waves of pleasure from the unicorn.

CHAPTER EIGHTEEN

If he had closed his eyes, Starbuck would not have known he and Magician were racing furiously through a tangled forest. Magician was surefooted and he avoided obstacles effortlessly. He seemed to pick out his route by a kind of internal radar, never stumbling, hardly even brushing a leaf when he hurtled through a narrow space between trees.

Starbuck could not get his last view of Megan out of his mind. He regretted that he had almost caused her to die as a result of his blunder, his botched less-than-heroic attempt at a rescue. He hoped Magician had received his sensory impression correctly, hoped that she was all right.

Magician: Of course she's all right.

She might be all right now, but her condition was definitely weak. Even if the Cylon shot had only grazed her, it would be just another contribution to her deteriorating state. There was no question about it; she had to be rescued, and soon. He could no longer wait for the *Galactica*'s search party to show up and help him storm the fortress. For that matter, what guarantee did he have they would *ever* show up? Something might have happened to Boomer. Starbuck didn't like the idea much, but he had to admit to himself it was possible. His comrade could have encountered more enemy ships and not even reached the home base. Even if he had, the situation aboard the *Galactica*—with the continuing threat of Cylons breaking through the fleet's erratic defensive force field, or of a destructive malfunction on any of the fleet's ships, or of any other disaster—might prevent the *Galactica* from sending a rescue party. The commander might even be forced to deem Starbuck expendable, dispatch no rescue ships. Anything could happen. And Starbuck did not have time to waste on waiting for an official rescue.

He could not attack the fortress alone—Spectre and his robotized Cylons were too numerous, the garrison close to impregnable. That left him with an unpalatable but practical course of action. He could use the children. He would have to ally with Kyle who had, after all, double-crossed him, lied to him, and delivered him as a gift package, wrapped, to the enemy. He did not like enlisting the aid of children, but it seemed the best and most feasible plan. Kyle's braggadocio might be a handicap, but he was a brave young man, and he did want Megan rescued, so he might just cooperate. He just might—

Magician came to an abrupt halt, almost heaving Starbuck over his bobbing head.

What is it?

Bad animal is near, sensing us. Very near. Stand on my back.

What—

Stand on my back. Pull yourself onto the large limb. Now!

Starbuck obeyed Magician quicker than he had ever obeyed an order from a superior on the *Galactica*. He pulled himself up to the branch, hung there for a moment, then worked his way around to the topside of the branch. The branch held his weight firmly. Beneath him Magician braced tensely, only his head moving, his slanted eyes searching the perimeter of the small clearing ahead for a clue to the whereabouts of the beast of prey.

He is on the other side. Watching. Watching me. He is ready to spring.

Magician was right. From out of the darkness, with

a leap that seemed impossible for such a massive and heavy animal, a lion sailed through the air across the clearing. Magician lowered his head and rushed toward his attacker. Clearly he aimed to impale the lion on his horn, but he just missed. The lion landed on the ground in front of Magician and immediately lunged for the unicorn's throat. Starbuck's stomach churned as he saw a small bloody chunk of Magician's hide come away in the lion's mouth. Magician twisted away, pranced sideways as if looking for an escape, then suddenly whirled on the lion and came at the beast from the side. Magician's horn cut a rip along the lion's flank that virtually tore the animal open from neck to tail. In a frenzied leap, the lion tore again at Magician's throat. This time its teeth went deeper and it was able to hold on, cling to the unicorn's throat. Magician, in a splendid rearing motion, rose on his hind legs, attempting to throw the lion off. Instead, the predator hung on, bouncing against Magician's hide like an ugly bloody necklace. As Magician came down, the lion finally released its grip, landed on its feet, and staggered backwards, toward the dark jungle from which he had materialized. Intending to find a warm place and die there, it appeared. But Magician wanted the beast to die now and he lowered his head, blood still streaming from his throat, and lunged toward the lion. With the last of its strength, the lion fell sideways, out of the unicorn's path. Magician could not stop—he kept galloping forward. He collided with a tree at the forest periphery, and his horn stuck there, deep in the bark. He tried to pull it out, struggling backwards furiously, but his wounds had drained the strength from his body and his strenuous efforts to remove the horn failed.

"Magician!" Starbuck called aloud.

The telepathic impression he received in response was faint, muddled. It had something to do with dying, but Starbuck could not understand it.

Then, his enormous body slumping, his horn still

imbedded in the tree bark, Magician did die. The flow of telepathic images in Starbuck's mind ended abruptly.

Starbuck, helpless, stuck on a tree branch, feeling that he had now failed twice in a row, yelled a long howl that resembled more the sound of an animal than a man.

CHAPTER NINETEEN

FROM MIRI'S BOOK:
After searching for Starbuck or Magician for a long
while, I finally heard the faraway noises of animals fighting. A moment later, as I rode toward the ferocious
sounds, I picked up a thought from Magician. Not a
thought so much as a surge of agony, a brief flash of
pain, the awareness of death coming, then an abrupt end
to the whole telepathic impression. After a moment of
quiet, with even the birds going silent, there was a long
pained howl, a man's howl. I became frightened that the
predator, having disposed of Magician, was now attack-
ing Starbuck. Get there, I thought to Rogue. Fast! Rogue
virtually flew through the forest ahead of us.

As I came into the clearing I saw first the corpse of
the lion. Its side had been ripped open, in a neat almost
surgical gash. Then the smell of blood showed me where
Magician was, hanging limp from the point where his
horn had become imbedded in a tree. Aside from the
bleeding wounds in his neck, Magician appeared peaceful.

I circled the clearing, looking for a sign of Starbuck.
I was so afraid that I'd find his corpse, too. When I
didn't see him anywhere, I thought that maybe he'd fled.
I looked for a trail, but the only track-signs I could find
were the ones that showed Magician coming to the clearing.

"Miri."

Starbuck's voice. I looked around again, still unable
to see him.

"Up here."

I followed the sound of his voice. Starbuck was sitting on a thick branch, most of his body obscured by its bushy leaves. His head seemed to float above me, bodiless. Then he jumped off the branch, landing beside Rogue. His eyes were saddened. He glanced toward Magician's body.

"There was nothing I could do. He planted me up there, *ordered* me onto that branch, left me helpless."

"He wanted to protect you."

"All I did was watch, all I—"

"There wasn't anything you could do. He had to battle his natural enemy. This lion must have been fierce. Magician's already killed many of them."

"Yeah, I suppose this is all natural to you. Animals and predators. I just, well, never cared much for a particular animal before. I wasn't much for—"

"I understand, Starbuck. I'm sad, too. I loved Magician. Sometimes he sent thoughts to me. I was glad when he chose you. And this isn't natural for me. Never."

I rode over to Magician and, taking out my knife, began cutting off his horn at the base.

"What are you doing?" Starbuck cried, running to me, shocked.

"The horn has curative powers. We will need it. The poultice I applied to your leg was begun with powder from the horn of a unicorn. This *is* natural. What are you looking so angry about?"

"I don't know, Miri. It seems—some kind of desecration of the body. To cut off a part of it while it's still warm. There's a kind of butchery in the—"

"Not at all, Starbuck. It's our custom. The unicorns understand it as well. Rogue, for example, is content, knowing that his comrade's death may help another life. His sadness is mixed with approval for removing Magician's horn."

As my knife swiftly slashed through the horn's base, Magician's body collapsed heavily to the ground. Starbuck knelt beside it. I could see in his eyes that he still hoped that Magician could receive his thoughts. I said nothing.

When Starbuck was ready, he stood up and said to me:

"Do we just leave him here?"

"I'm afraid so. We have no time. When we can, we bury them or cast them into deep water, which is the unicorn's chosen burial site, so they'll not be carrion for further predators. But we cannot do that now."

"Let's go back to camp."

I swung up onto Rogue's back.

"Rogue says it's all right for you to ride on him behind me."

"Tell him thanks."

After we had ridden for a while, with me feeling a strong awareness of Starbuck's presence behind me, even of areas where necessity did not force us to touch, Starbuck said suddenly:

"We have to make plans."

"Plans?"

"I'm afraid for your mother."

He told me of an attempt to rescue Megan and how she'd been wounded.

"She may be too weak for us to leave her in that blasted cell any longer. I was waiting for my buddies from the *Galactica* to arrive. However, it's occurred to me there's a good chance they may *never* get here. So we have to attack immediately. Tonight, if possible."

"We have to attack? You mean Kyle's band?"

"That's what I'm thinking."

"But they're just children, you said so yourself."

"I realize what I said."

"They could get killed."

"I realize that, too."

"But you can't just despatch them like that, like a real army. They're not really an army, no matter how much Kyle struts or how much they enjoy their little raids."

"Believe me, I realize *all* of that, Miri. My plans don't call for them getting killed. I'm trying to work out a way to attack the fortress and not have *anybody* killed. Nobody but Cylons anyway. And these Cylons are just machines."

"And just how do you plan to do that?"

"Give me time to think. I have the beginning of a strategy, if only I can work out the details."

I was as furious with Starbuck as I usually was with Kyle when he started such warlike talk.

"What? Arm the children, give them guns and let them shoot their way in?"

I could hear Starbuck laughing quietly behind me, and, more than before, was aware of his arms around my waist. Acutely aware.

"No, that's not the way. My thinking was running more in the line of children's games."

"Children's games! But—"

"Quiet, Miri. Let me think. I may be on to something."

I did not know what to think. But I was afraid.

Before we entered camp, Starbuck asked me to stop. We both dismounted, to give the overworked Rogue a much needed rest, for which he sent me waves of gratitude. Standing beside Rogue, Starbuck interrogated me for a long time. He wanted to know the layout of the Cylon garrison, the location of the tower, the dimensions of the secret passage, the whereabouts of the command room, and many other details I didn't even know I remembered until his questions.

Then we rode into camp. Jergin was the first to see us, and her pretty face broke into a bright smile.

"We thought you boondogglers were never coming back," she said, running to us. I dismounted and hugged her.

Soon all the children were gathered around us, asking what had happened. Kyle hung back, his face morose.

Starbuck's voice broke several times, first as he told of Megan's physical condition, then when he described the failure of his rescue attempt, and finally—on the brink of tears—when he described the death of Magician. Some of the older children were visibly affected by his narrative, while many of the younger ones treated it all as a story and stared wide-eyed at Starbuck as if he were merely telling tales around a campfire. When he had finished, there was a long silence. Finally, Ariadne whispered:

"Mother . . . what will happen to mother?"

Nilz touched Starbuck's arm and tears rolled down from his eyes as he said:

"They'll . . . kill her this time, won't they?"

Starbuck glanced at me, then responded to Nilz gently:

"No, they won't kill her. I think even they know how valuable she is to them. They'll want to keep her alive, maybe bargain again to stop your raids."

"Are you sure, Starbuck?" Ariadne asked.

"Of course I'm sure."

But I could tell by the catch in his voice as he said it that he was not at all sure. He told the children to gather around and gestured Kyle forward.

"Megan is all right now, but we can't wait much longer. Can't let her waste away in that tower. I have some ideas about—"

"No, Starbuck!" Kyle interrupted.

"Kyle, I'm on your side. Please don't get your nose out of joint again."

"Starbuck, before we discuss your ideas, I have something to say. Publicly. The exchange was a grave tactical error. I see that now. I'm relinquishing my command to you."

Starbuck's reaction to Kyle's offer was clearly mixed. His eyes were sad, but he was also on the verge of smiling.

"I'm trying not to fight you for command, Kyle," he

said quietly. "I never intended to."

"I understand. But it is important that . . . certain procedures take place. I'm no longer fit for command. I want it official that you take over leadership."

Kyle stared at Starbuck, his eyes desperately eager for the pilot's response. And approval. Slowly, Starbuck nodded.

"Okay, scout, I'll accept. But on one condition."

"Name it."

Starbuck went to Kyle, put his right hand on Kyle's shoulder, and said softly:

"That you be my lieutenant."

Kyle grinned. He could not help it. It was the first warm smile I'd seen from him since I don't know when. It made me smile, too.

"With pleasure, sir," Kyle said, his stiff body displaying his pride. He could not quite avoid the habits of pomposity even in his new subordinate role. "What are your orders?"

Starbuck paused, then addressed everyone:

"Tonight we will organize to infiltrate the Cylon encampment and rescue Megan."

At first there were cheers, and Starbuck spread his hands to quiet down the excited children.

"Now don't get overexcited. The important thing you all must remember is to be calm, at least as calm as possible under the circumstances. First, we must make plans."

"Shall I prepare to dispense weapons?" Kyle asked.

"No. We're not going to use guns if we can help it."

Kyle looked scared.

"But it's dangerous to go up against the Cylons without weapons."

"Oh, we'll have weapons. They just won't be rifles and pistols, that's all. Anybody here good with a slingshot?"

"I am!" Ariadne shouted eagerly.

"Do I have a job for you!"

Ariadne was pleased.

"Starbuck," Kyle protested, "we can't go against them with slingshots!"

"Not only slingshots, but jump ropes, tin whistles, balloons, bubble pipes, whatever—maybe a few good old-fashioned and well-aimed rocks."

"I don't understand," Kyle said weakly.

"I'm not saying we'll be entirely weaponless. But I won't allow young children to fight this battle with laser weapons and bombs."

"They've used them before."

"But not under my command."

Kyle looked angry enough to take back his offer of relinquishing leadership.

"And we're not children!" he cried.

"You've said that before. But you know deep-down as well as I do that you are children. All of you."

"Starbuck—"

"*All* of you, Kyle."

Kyle's shoulder's slumped. The gesture was a kind of admission of the truth, or at least as close to one as Kyle could get.

"I'll make this one concession. Some of you, the more able among the older children, will be allowed to *carry* weapons. But to be used only for defensive purposes or to help the younger ones. Let's see. Laughing Jake, I think you can handle yourself with that pistol you're already toting. And Herbert, you can requisition a weapon from supply. And Jergin, you'd better arm yourself.

Starbuck paused. Kyle looked sheepish. Starbuck smiled.

"And of course Kyle. You'll *have* to have a weapon, to make your disguise look accurate."

Kyle grinned, then frowned.

"Disguise?" he said.

"Kyle, my boy." Kyle flinched slightly at the word *boy*, but nodded anyway. "Kyle, you're going to be a starfleet warrior tonight. In full regalia. You are, in fact, going to be Lieutenant Starbuck of the Battlestar *Galactica*."

Kyle beamed with pride.

Starbuck picked up a stick and began drawing a rough map of the garrison on the ground.

"Now listen carefully. Each of you will have a job. I figured you'd all been playing war games long enough. You haven't had enough time for children's games, so I remembered some from my youth. We're going to use a few of them."

Kyle came to my side and smiled. I locked my arm in his, and we waited for Starbuck to present the drill.

CHAPTER TWENTY

Lucifer, gliding into the command room, was greeted by an excited and abnormally cheerful Baltar. The human's spirits had certainly revived considerably since he had first discovered the existence of Spectre—a computer after his own heart, as he once called him in one of his many attempts to annoy Lucifer. It did annoy Lucifer that Baltar's verbal thrusts were succeeding more often than they should have.

"Another transmission from Antila, Lucifer. Right on schedule, as always. Here's old Spectre now."

Lucifer was amazed at how childish Baltar sometimes became when he was in an excitable mood.

"I apologize for the delay, honored sir," Spectre said as soon as his image had formed on the screen. "I am afraid I have to report setbacks. Temporary, of course, but setbacks nevertheless."

"Yes, go on. I'm sure your reasons are sound, Spectre."

As sound as a discarded battery, Lucifer thought.

"The captured warrior is still unconscious," Spectre said. "I am afraid—I'm afraid he could even . . . terminate."

"Die!"

Lucifer was surprised by Baltar's sudden angry reaction. The first moment of displeasure with Spectre. A good sign, a very good sign.

"Unfortunately, sir," Spectre said, "my unit is prog— is enthusiastic about their duties. They can be a shade too rough on the enemy. It may be that their knowledge of human anatomy is too limited."

Baltar nodded.

"That is unfortunate. But I understand fully. The exigencies of war sometimes force extreme actions."

"Still, sir, I do not offer excuses. Despite my securing this planet in what I may without modesty say was accomplished with great efficiency and speed, if it should happen that this warrior does terminate, then I can only say I have failed completely. Myself and my mission would be total failures. For, in failing you, Baltar, I will have failed one of the great leaders of our task force."

Lucifer recalled an expression of Starbuck's, which he now muttered to himself: "The felgercarb is so thick you couldn't fly a viper through it." He was not sure exactly what the expression meant, but it did seem to apply to Spectre's open flattery of Baltar. Apparently Baltar liked felgercarb, for he answered Spectre gently:

"Now, don't be too hard on yourself. From the reports I've read, you've done a brilliant job there and I may add a few laudatory comments to your next efficiency report."

Once again, Lucifer was glad he was not human, since what he would've done at that moment would have terribly messed up the command room floor.

"I do not know what to say, honored sir. Of course I will continue to do my best and I will spare no effort to save this pilot's life, at least long enough to extract the information you seek."

"I ask no less, Spectre. I know you're a—a computer of your word."

"Thank you, sir. By your command."

"Goodbye, Spectre."

Spectre's image faded to dots, then vanished from the screen. Lucifer could not resist saying:

"You actually believed all of that . . . fantasy."

Baltar said in an oily voice:

"Lucifer, this jealousy is simply not like you. Perhaps you need an overhaul, a restructuring of your programming. Spectre is doing a fine job and he will receive the proper commendations, in spite of your petty envy."

Lucifer decided not to carry the issue any further. After all, Baltar's threat to change his programming might just be genuine. Lucifer could wind up as underhanded and as foolish as Spectre.

With a trained scientific detachment, Spectre watched life come back into Megan's eyes. She had been staring lifelessly at him for some time and at least twice he had been certain that she had died, then awareness seemed to sweep across both her eyes. Of course the reason for the effect was that she had been in a daze, virtually unconscious, and now she was awake, conscious of him staring down at her. From the look of hatred in her eyes, he deduced that he was the last being of any kind that she wanted to see at this moment.

She glanced down at the dressing which Hilltop had hastily applied, after carrying her himself into the command room.

"Your shoulder is adequately repaired," Spectre said. "I am sorry we have such meager medical capability. For humans, at least. But that bandage should at least keep your bodily oil inside, and I believe there are no dangers to your life. My warriors, I am afraid, could be somewhat better shots than they are."

Megan glared at him. Clearly she did not understand much of what he said. It looked to Spectre as if the woman would not survive much longer, but it would not be the wound that killed her—it would be something else, something too human for him to understand.

"I'm all right," she whispered. "Your aide's work was . . . efficient. He learns quickly. He had to tear the blouse. Pity. I liked the blouse. I told him that. He apologized, I thought that was quite unique in a Cylon. Apologies."

Her voice seemed to be drifting off, fading. It was obvious that she could not concentrate on what was said to her.

"I told him not to be sorry. He followed my orders very well about how to treat the wound. Miri would have done better, of course. But your aide has medical abilities. Very capable, for a tincan."

Spectre glanced at Hilltop, who was steadily keeping his own gaze elsewhere. Although there was no way Hilltop could have displayed embarrassment, there was nevertheless a definite aura of uneasiness around him. What would cause such an effect? Spectre wondered. Had he constructed his creations more effectively than he had suspected? Or had he made *this* one somehow better than the others? He would have to disassemble Hilltop at the first opportunity to obtain clues about what made him different from the others.

"What did you learn from the colonial warrior, Megan?" Spectre asked.

Megan looked puzzled.

"*What* colonial warrior?"

Then she appeared to remember.

"Oh, him. Aren't I supposed not to tell? Isn't that the warrior's code? Name, rank, classification number. His name's Starbuck, I can tell you that."

Starbuck. Well, that was more information about the pilot than Spectre had previously obtained.

"But I really learned little else about him, little of value to you anyway. You'd waste time trying to find out any more. He's a . . . a pleasant man. For a soldier. He's got misgivings. I could almost like him. Miri likes him. You like him."

"I like him? I hardly saw the man."

Megan's eyes were dazed again.

"Did I say you? I meant Kyle. How did I get you confused with Kyle? I don't even know why I would have said Kyle. I never saw Kyle this time. But Starbuck seemed sympathetic to Kyle, to the children. I liked Starbuck, I told you that. You would like to hear more about him?"

"No, I believe I would not. Take her back to the cell."

Hilltop started to pick her up and carry her to the tower himself.

"Hilltop!"

"Yes, honored sir?"

"I did not mean for you to take her back. You are command personnel. You leave such jobs to menial personnel."

"If you insist. But I would not object to carrying—"

"Give her to the guards, Hilltop!"

Hilltop obeyed in his usual brisk manner. A pair of centurions took charge of Megan and took her away. Still, Spectre thought, Hilltop's offer to take charge of Megan himself seemed definitely aberrant. Yes, he would have to take Hilltop apart one of these days. If he could ever get the time.

He considered whether to transmit to Baltar again, this time admitting the truth, that he had only had the warrior in custody for a brief time and it appeared he might never capture him again. Baltar was so conciliatory, he might treat an admission of failure lightly. He was human, after all, not Cylon. Yet, he was crafty, and he did follow Cylon rules. No, it would not do Spectre any good to admit failure to a human or a Cylon. But Spectre did not feel hopeful. Since the pilot had already slipped through his manipulative digits once, Spectre wondered if he was fated ever to capture this—what had Megan called him?—this Starbuck.

Hilltop broke into his meditation by shouting:

"Sir! It's the warrior. He's . . . he's outside the garrison walls."

"What? We've captured him?"

"No. He is just there, outside the walls, astride a white unicorn. Just sitting on his mount and staring at the walls. Waving to us."

"Waving?"

"Yes, should we kill him?"

"No, by all means. We must capture him alive. Send a patrol out to take custody of him."

"Yes, sir, I have a patrol waiting."

Spectre followed Hilltop out of the command room. Taking a ramp he had ordered specially built for him, he glided up to the platform that ran all around the inside of the walls to see the phenomenon for himself. The warrior was, indeed, out there. And he was, indeed, waving. Not a wave exactly. A challenge of some sort.

"Do you surrender, human?" Spectre shouted, as the garrison gates opened and the patrol, holding their rifles forward, marched out.

"Not on your life, bulbhead."

Spectre almost ordered the man shot for the insult. But he needed him alive, if only to display him to Baltar and Lucifer.

"Bring him to me," he shouted at the patrol.

"It'll take more warriors than that to subdue me. C'mon, fellas, we're gonna play follow the leader."

The white unicorn reared and started for the forest.

"Get him!" Spectre shouted.

The patrol pursued their quarry into the forest. Spectre watched for a long time, eventually became tired of seeing nothing but landscape, and was about to turn and return to the command room where he belonged in such a crisis, when the man on the white unicorn appeared again at the forest edge. This time he looked different, smaller. Was it possible there were two colonial warriors crashed on the planet?

"Not good enough, bulbhead," the warrior shouted. "It's gonna take more of your rattletrap soldiers to catch me."

"Send out more warriors," Spectre said to Hilltop, "a larger patrol."

"Are you sure that is wise, sir, to deplete personnel like—"

"Do what I say, Hilltop."

As he watched Hilltop assemble the larger patrol, Spectre imagined the step-by-step procedures he would take in disassembling an aide who was obviously on the verge of malfunction.

The colonial warrior waited for a time at the edge of the forest, then bolted back into the darkness when the gates opened again and the new patrol emerged, this time firing their weapons.

CHAPTER TWENTY-ONE

FROM MIRI'S BOOK:
We all searched out hiding places in the trees, behind bushes, under arched tree roots, while Jergin took charge of taking the mounts back to a safe clearing. Only Demon was left behind, on Starbuck's orders.

The Cylon garrison looked peaceful. Guards, walking slowly, patrolled the platform at the top of the wall. It seemed ironic to me that a wall built originally by the colonists to keep predators out of the settlement now functioned as protection for the predators who had taken over the settlement.

In an area just in front of the garrison gates, a few tincans worked at a task that made no sense to me. It seemed to involve them each taking pieces of themselves and exchanging them for other parts which they then put into, upon, or against themselves. Perhaps it was their kind of game, perhaps it was a religious ritual.

Starbuck sent Melysa and Nilz, our most adept climbers, scampering up a pair of strategically-located trees. They observed from high perches for a while, as commanded, then came down with the report that inside the garrison everything looked routine, Cylons performing Cylonish activities. Melysa said she thought she saw Megan, escorted by centurions, entering the door to the prison tower. Starbuck questioned Melysa and Nilz at length and in detail, concentrating especially on information regarding the number of warriors and their observable armaments.

"There are too many of them inside there, that's certain," he said finally to Kyle and me. "We can't lead in any kind of group through the secret passage and expect to make it across the courtyard unobserved. As it stands now, it's a sucker's move."

"It may be impregnable," Kyle muttered, discouraged.

"I didn't say that."

"Starbuck, when the tincans invaded, the colony held out a long time, before the Cylons finally crashed through with their superior firepower. We were already evacuating through the secret passage when the massacre started. That's why mostly children got out. There're always two or three score of the tincans roaming about the yard. Sure, Miri can sneak in once in a while, work her way across the yard to the tower, but a whole attack squad, never. We wouldn't stand a chance."

"Ah, but we haven't begun our games yet."

"Starbuck—"

"Have faith, Kyle, have faith. It's time for phase one. Or the first move, if you want to preserve the gaming metaphor."

"Of course we'll try."

"That's the spirit. I'm encouraged by your doubts. A little caution never hurt any strategy. Okay, like I told you, be ready for the quick-change when I return."

"I hope I can manage to look like you to them."

"Of course you will. They can't tell us apart anyway. Hold Demon, while I get on him. I want him to know you approve, Kyle."

Kyle stroked Demon's neck while Starbuck mounted to his back. Demon accepted Starbuck as rider without any perceivable qualm. I don't know if Kyle was pleased or not.

"Well, folks," Starbuck said to those of us gathered around him, "the first stage of gameplaying is the challenge. At least one person must challenge at least one opponent. Except for solitaire, and solitaire never

brought anybody any chips. Think I'll go out there and
hustle up some action. Those of you with phase-one
duties, go to your positions."

Starbuck rode out to the clearing in front of the garrison, and started shouting and waving in a berserk fashion. My heart started beating rapidly. I prayed that none
of the guards would get anxious and start shooting at
him. For this first part of his strategy to work, he had
to be right when he said they would want him bad enough
not to kill him outright.

There was a great deal of commotion and confusion
along the garrison walls after they had seen Starbuck on
Demon. Finally, Spectre came to the platform and returned Starbuck's challenge by inviting him to surrender.
Starbuck mocked him and wheeled Demon around, riding him back into the forest. After considerable cacoph-
onous noise inside the garrison, the gates opened and
a patrol came rushing out, racing past the tin cans that
had been exchanging parts, who seemed to see no logic
in what was happening around them.

Meanwhile, Starbuck rode Demon up to us and dismounted in a hurry. Quickly he took off his flight jacket
and trousers, exchanging them for Kyle's outfit. Kyle's
forest clothes fit Starbuck snugly, while the starfleet
uniform hung a little loosely on Kyle. The clothing had
been exchanged before I realized that I had watched it
all without an ounce of embarrassment. I had been living
with an outlaw band in the forest too long for modesty
to hold much sway over me, I suppose.

Kyle leaped onto Demon and rode away. He deliberately placed himself in the patrol's path, made sure he
was observed, and raced off.

"First game: Follow the leader," Starbuck muttered.
"That's it, guys, you're all playing it just fine."

The patrol was soon out of sight. The Genie asked
Starbuck if they should now start sneaking into the secret
passage.

"Yes, a few at a time," he answered, "but wait for Miri and me before going exploring. All right?"

"Yes, sir!"

"And you can drop the military courtesy. This is a keepers game and there's no time for frills."

The Genie nodded stoically and went off to organize the children who were assigned to the passage. I sensed them sneaking into the entrance under the bush but—to give them credit—I did not actually observe a single member of the squad enter. Starbuck had stayed in the darkness at the edge of the forest, awaiting Kyle's return and keeping a lookout on the garrison walls, where Spectre remained, the red lights of his eyes scanning the landscape in front of him.

Although I feared unplanned-for complications, in my mind I imagined this part of the operation working perfectly. I saw Kyle leading the patrol deeper into the forest, where the children delegated to the ambush detail waited up in trees, tangled in greenery, and in any other position that gave them sudden-attack leverage. I imagined Robus and Nilz, who had the only jump rope we could scavenge, waiting for the patrol to pass, then tripping up the rearguard Cylons and kicking away their weapons, while other children jumped from their positions onto, against, and beneath the rest of the patrol, making the tincans fall all over each other in confusion. Then, as the ambushers skittered out of the way, the net hurriedly sewn by Ariadne's seamstress-platoon would be spread over the fallen Cylons by the remaining members of the detail. Leaving a couple of children to stand guard over the secured and unresistant Cylons (Starbuck's theory, proven correct, was that the tincans would malfunction under pressure), Kyle would return to us.

Before I could recall all the details of this phase, Kyle *had* returned to us, with the news that the ambush had worked like clockwork. He looked to Starbuck for the signal to begin phase two. Starbuck gave it, and Kyle went just to the edge of the forest, where he would be sufficiently in shadow not to be easily recognized as a substitute for Starbuck. Kyle shouted the second challenge, as instructed him by Starbuck.

"Game two," Starbuck muttered. "A variation of blind man's buff. The underwater version this time, fellows, give or take some mud."

Starbuck and I ducked as the second patrol, larger in number, crashed out of the garrison gates with the weapons at the ready and firing. Beams of laser light seemed to be everywhere above us.

Kyle laughed brashly as he and Demon rode off, this time in a different direction than before, the patrol following at their clumsy but amazingly rapid pace.

As soon as they were out of sight, Starbuck whispered:

"Okay, Miri, time to join the others in the tunnel. This game is called, let's see, the maze. It's a paper kind of game, really. We enter here, point A with an arrow, and make our way through tunnels and past obstacles, trying not to get caught in any of the deadends or traps, in order to find the true way to our objective, in this case the prison tower, point B or whatever."

I shuddered involuntarily.

"I'm not sure I really like treating all this as a game," I said. "Especially this part of it."

Starbuck regarded me sympathetically.

"I expect you wouldn't. You're right, Miri. But I'm really trying to protect the children by making a game out of this. It's a lot better than sending them in with guns and bombs, and training them to think of themselves in heroic terms. Maybe just as dangerous, but I suspect we can make it work, you and I. That's part of our job, really, protecting the children while we rescue your mother and the other prisoners. We can do it."

"I wish I could be so confident."

"You been in as many scrapes as I have, you learn how to fake confidence."

"But you're brave."

Starbuck smiled.

"So are you, Miri. C'mon, into the tunnel."

I almost looked for the arrow saying point A as I sneaked beneath the bush as I had done so many times before, with Starbuck right behind me.

CHAPTER TWENTY-TWO

Kyle had some trouble holding down Demon's speed so that the Cylon pursuers could keep him in sight. Demon did stick firmly to the zigzag pattern that kept the Cylons from getting off a good shot at them, although a few leaves uncomfortably close to Kyle's head were singed in passing.

The zigzag move was Kyle's addition to Starbuck's plan. The individual Cylons each had a fairly good directional system and they might be able to discern where Kyle was heading too soon. Erratic trails, however, tended to confuse the tincans, or at least Kyle was counting on that. The zigzagging did seem to be working. The patrol showed no awareness of how close they were to the dangerous swampy area. He hoped that the children assigned to this detail had devised, as ordered, an effective camouflage. He had not had time to go there and inspect their work.

"All right, Demon," he whispered aloud. "I think we've just about netted these guys. We'll make our move in just a while."

For the first time since he had begun riding Demon, Kyle received a telepathic message from him, a wave of agreement and the information that the timing of the final jump could be left up to Demon himself. Kyle felt elated. After all this time, Demon had finally broken his mental silence.

Why? Kyle wondered.

Had to wait until I was sure you would listen, came Demon's response. All right, this is it, time for the final run.

Demon broke out of the zigzag pattern as he reached a wide trail. At first he cantered slowly, to give the Cylons an opportunity to catch up. When they had reached the path and started to propel themselves faster toward Kyle and his unicorn, Demon increased the pace. Kyle looked back.

Good, he thought, they're going faster, too.

Demon accelerated to a fast trot, but Kyle thought: Slower, they're beginning to fall behind again. We have to make sure they maintain their top speed, or else they'll be able to stop in time. Demon understood and kept the rate of speed just right. On the open road the Cylons could move much more swiftly. These robotized versions were fast, and their lighter weight allowed them to be speedier than genuine Cylons.

Okay, Demon, I think we've reached the point of no return. As soon as we get around that curve, you—

Let me judge that. Just a little more time.

You're cutting it pretty thin.

It is necessary.

Demon began trotting faster, working up speed for the jump-to-come. Rounding the curve, briefly out of sight of their pursuers, Kyle saw the camouflage ahead. At the point where the road actually came to an abrupt end at the edge of the swamp, the children had been able to paint on dried animal hide a good illusion of a road, one that seemed to proceed a little further, then curved into a gradual right turn. He was sure the Cylons would be fooled. He almost was. He did not have time to see if Goodchild and Arno Armwaver, two of the strongest among the younger children, were securely in position so that they could jerk the camouflage away in time.

For a moment it looked as if Demon might time his jump a shade too late—but, no, he had the move down pat. When it seemed that they were going to run smack into the camouflage and spoil the whole plan, Demon lifted suddenly into the air, sailing over the rather high hurdle that was the top of the camouflage-painting. They

came down sharply on the other side, Demon's front
hooves landing just short of the beginning of the swampy
area. Kyle could see reflections in the muddy water a
few feet below, down the steep bank. It felt for a moment
as if Kyle would be pitched forward, but Demon was
in control. As soon as his rear hooves touched ground,
he was leaping again, this time sideways and into a thick
patch of jungle, where he and Kyle would be temporarily
concealed as the Cylons rushed past. In a perfectly timed
move, just before the swift Cylon warriors, now accel-
erating because they did not have their quarry in sight,
had reached the barrier of the road-painting, Goodchild
and Arno pulled it up and away. The momentum of the
patrol leader carried him forward, and the patrol, obe-
dient warriors all, followed right after. By the time he
had reached the edge of the bank, and his sensors had
perceived that there was only swampy and muddy water
ahead, it was too late, he could not halt his forward
propulsion. He fell down the steep bank, tumbling metal
head over metal heels. All but two of the rest of the
patrol stumbled right off the bank on top of him. As they
came in contact with the water, without the time to protect themselves in any way from its harming effects,
sparks started to fly. The water gradually covered them.
Other warriors were not affected by the water and were
able to partially recover and stand up, but were trapped
by the underlying mud which Kyle knew was, in this
part of the swamp, virtually quicksand. Their movements to squirm out of the mud only sank them deeper.
The leader, flat on his back in the water but still functioning, called an indiscernible squeaky order to the two
centurions who had avoided falling off the bank. His
words were obviously commands to lend a hand, rescue
them. The two centurions seemed confused, but their
bewilderment did not last long, for Goodchild and Arno
Armwaver sneaked up behind them and, laughing glee-
fully, pushed the centurions into the water. A warrior
imbedded in muck but with his arms free, raised his

weapon, aimed it at Goodchild. Kyle, reacting quickly, had his pistol out. He shot the rifle out of the Cylon's hand. The rifle fell into the water and its subsequent short-circuiting sent a chain reaction of electrical waves from Cylon to Cylon. Soon they all seemed to have malfunctioned. They fell against each other and soon looked like a floating junkpile.

The trick had worked better than Starbuck, with Kyle's aid, had planned. Kyle rode out from his hiding place and told Goodchild and Arno Armwaver that they did not have to post a guard.

"Let's go back, see if we can help the others," Kyle ordered.

Megan drifted in and out of sleep. When awake, she discovered that her problem with focussing her eyes had become worse. She could make out little that was distinct, and she found it better to sleep. She wanted to sleep, and that was all she wanted right now, maybe all she would ever want from now on. Dimly, the pains in her shoulder throbbed, felt like a miniature ballet ensemble laboriously rehearsing a new and difficult piece of choreography all along her nerves.

Once she awoke and Kordel was standing over her. She could see him distinctly, no blurred edges—so distinctly that she wondered if perhaps this was merely a dream. How perverse, to dream of the cell she lived in, the straw bed on which she slept.

Kordel's eyes were unusually concerned.

"I don't think you're going to make it, Megan," he whispered kindly. "Something's happening to your wound, your dressing is bloodier than it was when that ugly tincan brought you back here."

"I'm . . . all right. I just want to sleep."

"Don't sleep. Try to get up, walk around maybe."

"Had . . . enough exercise . . . went on a trip . . . let me sleep."

"Try to sit up."

He took her hands in his and pulled her to a sitting position but, no matter how much he struggled with her, that was as far as she could go.

"Can't, Kordel. Let me sleep, please."

"Damn them!" he muttered bitterly. "Here, let me see if I can bind that dressing any tighter." He stood up, called to the other prisoners of the cell block, "Anybody here got any bandages, any medical equipment?" He was answered by silence. "I need some strips of cloth, anything." The silence remained, but it was interrupted by the sounds of ripping cloth.

Soon Kordel was holding several soiled fraying strips of cloth, passed along from several prisoners. Carefully he started working at Megan's dressing. Soon he was cursing himself. There seemed nothing he could do to stem the small but steady flow of blood out of the wound. As he tried to press his makeshift bandaging tighter against the wound. Megan slipped easily again into unconsciousness, mumbling something odd about a ballet company and how they were never going to get it right.

CHAPTER TWENTY-THREE

FROM MIRI'S BOOK:
"Miri," Starbuck exclaimed, "this isn't just a secret passage. It's a labyrinth, a *real* maze. I've seen catacombs that looked like simple caves compared to this!"

For some illogical reason, I was pleased by his astonished remarks.

"I'm so used to following my one route, Starbuck, that I'd forgotten how many corridors there were down here. Now I remember how long it took to find that route, how many times I found myself in blocked off corridors, dead-ends, or passages that were of no use to me."

In the torchlight, the uneven craggy surface of the passage's walls suggested all the dangers we were heading toward. Starbuck had asked me to lead, while he followed directly behind. The children, as ordered by Starbuck, lingered behind and came forward in surges at his command.

As we passed the room that hid all we had salvaged from the settlement museum, I said to Starbuck:

"The woman on the unicorn painting is in there. We hid away a lot of our art."

"Hope I get a chance to look at it."

The air inside the passage was still and cold. Colder than I'd ever remembered, or else my imagination, out of fear, was making it feel colder to me.

At last we came to the fireplace entrance. I explained to Starbuck how it worked.

"Let me reconnoiter first, see there's nobody in the warehouse," I said.

"No, I'll do it. I'm the—"

"I'm smaller and I'm used to it. I know the terrain, remember? *My* job."

"Good point."

Sliding the fireplace panel sideways, I scanned the immediate area in my usual fashion. I saw nothing. However, a thud on the other side of the first row of boxes told me there was somebody else in the warehouse.

"Wait here," I whispered.

"Be careful, Miri."

"Always."

I tiptoed to a pile of boxes near where the sound had originated. Peeking around them, I saw two tincans opening cartons. I reported back to Starbuck.

"Two of them. Working on cartons."

"Okay. We don't want to attract the attention of anybody from outside. Ariadne?"

"Yes, Starbuck?"

"I'll need you. Herbert and Jake, too."

"Right."

My hands felt odd. I looked down at them. They were trembling. I didn't remember trembling before.

"Starbuck?" I said.

"What is it, Miri?"

Ariadne, Jake, and Herbert reported for duty. I did not like the look of fun in Ariadne's clear green eyes.

"The cartons the tincans are opening," I said. "They were never there before. I think they hold rifles."

"Interesting. Somebody's ordered out more arms. We must be spooking them. Good."

"What's good about it?"

"It means our diversions are working. Okay, Ariadne, got your trusty slingshot?"

She held it up for him to see.

"Okay, you know what to do."

"Sure, Starbuck."

I wished I could be as confident as twelve-year-old Ariadne looked and sounded.

"Jake," Starbuck said. "We'll use the clubs here, you and I. Not a good spot for pistols. Remember the drill?"

"Yep, Starbuck."

Starbuck motioned for me to slide open the fireplace panel. He looked out cautiously, then crept forward, gesturing Ariadne, Herbert, and Jake to follow. I took up the rear, telling the other children to stay put.

They reached a pile of boxes which Starbuck looked around. The tincans were still there. They had stacked many rifles already. Starbuck nodded toward Ariadne, who—after Jake had given her a lift—nimbly climbed to a place atop a pile of boxes. She drew out her sling-shot, squinted her eyes to take careful aim, put a stone in the wellworn pouch of the elastic band (I recalled finding that elastic band for her in this very warehouse), pulled the sling back, and fired. The stone bounced off a Cylon shoulder with a small pinging sound. Ariadne scrunched down as the Cylon glanced upward and saw nothing. He went back to work. Ariadne placed another pellet into the sling and flung it. This one landed at the back of the other Cylon's leg. Same small ping. The two struck Cylons looked at each other, the red lights in their helmets moving almost in synchronicity. A third shot, hitting the first Cylon again, in his back. The two of them started hollering things to each other in that bizarre nasally-metallic speech. They arrived at their decision and began clumsily to walk in our direction, each of them holding up one of the unpacked rifles, ready to fire. I thought my heart had stopped beating. Starbuck and Herbert edged sideways, pressing against the boxes. Jake crouched on the other side of the narrow space the Cylons were approaching.

After they had passed without seeing any of us, Herbert and Jake jumped on the lead Cylon, while Starbuck attacked the other. After shoving the tincans down, Starbuck and Jake performed the maneuver they had planned during the briefing. They each raised their clubs and hit terrific blows against the lower chests of each

Cylon. As Starbuck had predicted, the robots' power packs were located there and the blows sent the tincans out of commission. They lay silent, now just piles of metal that, even if repaired, would never be the same beings.

"How did you know the power packs were there?" I whispered to Starbuck as we all cautiously made our way to the warehouse entrance.

"I got a chance to inspect one for a long time in the forest before you guys found me. I told you about that."

"But what if the power packs hadn't been located there?"

"Then we would have had to improvise."

"Starbuck, you're not exactly building up my confidence in you."

He stopped, held both my arms.

"Miri, I'd like for this to be easy. Of course there are risks. I'm conscious of them. And, believe me, if I see we're in extreme danger, I'll surrender."

"Surrender?"

"Yes, that's my ultimate contingency plan. If you and the children are hopelessly trapped, I'll give myself up. They really want *me* anyway. Their commander needs me for his service record, I think. That'll give you and the others a chance to hide or get away while the Cylons are fussing over me. So, see? I've got it all covered."

"But Starbuck, I don't want to sacrifice you."

"It'd be in a good cause. Now, c'mon, your job—what's next?"

"I'll check the courtyard."

The number of tincans in the yard was obviously depleted. Still, there seemed too many of them for our team to get across to the tower successfully. While I made my observation, I heard Kyle's voice coming from outside the garrison gates. He was challenging the Cylons again. Right on schedule. Starbuck's order for this maneuver was that Kyle should lead the next patrol on a merry chase. He was not even sure they would bite a third time, he had said. He had been wrong. They bit.

A tincan officer rushed out of the command room and assembled still another patrol. The gates were opened, Kyle whooped and blew his hunting horn, and I heard the sound of Demon galloping.

"What do you think, Miri?" Starbuck asked after the gates had closed.

"Still a lot of tincans out there. But fewer than usual. I think the three of us can make it."

"Okay. Jake, you ready?"

"Ready."

"Herbert, you know your job. Get to the fuel dump and wait for the signal from Jake's torch. A circle. Then hurl the bombs and get out of the way. The rest of you, be ready here. You all know what to do and you all know the contingency plans."

The children nodded together, as if all controlled from the same source. Starbuck told me to proceed.

Opening the warehouse door slowly, I slipped out first, then Starbuck, then Jake. As we moved from dark place to dark place, I noticed that I had never seen the yard in such chaos before. The tincans didn't seem to know what to do next, didn't even seem sure of what they were doing at the moment. I wondered if our diversions were bewildering them, maybe putting them on the verge of malfunction.

Suddenly Spectre appeared in the command room doorway, his outline highlighted and given an extra blue aura by the bizarre Cylon lighting behind him. I gestured for the others to halt. Spectre appeared to stare right at us, and I thought the game might be up, all our games might be up, but I suppose it was just my imagination working overtime, for Spectre turned around and reentered the command building.

I gestured for Starbuck and Jake to stay back while I checked out the first floor of the tower. We were lucky. None of the tincan guards were on ground level, although I heard some of them clanking around above me.

I also thought I heard Megan groaning, and I almost panicked right then and there.

Starbuck and Jake, running low, raced to the tower doorway across open area, and slipped in behind me. Jake stayed by the door, looking out.

"Nobody saw us," he informed Starbuck.

Starbuck drew his laser pistol and said to me:

"Okay, Miri, up to you and me now. Be ready to duck if a Cylon gets in front of us. Lead the way."

Leaving Jake behind to stand watch, I led Starbuck up the narrow iron staircase. We climbed it as carefully as we could, every little metal squeak sending waves of fright through my body. Apparently the Cylons inside the tower were as discombobulated as the ones outside. Not one of them heard our approach.

On the first cell block level, where Megan's cell was located, two guards were busily taking food trays off a cart and sliding them under cell doors. I was surprised that nobody in the cells paid any attention to their food. No-one made so much as a move toward a tray.

I tried to control my breathing. The air inside the tower seemed thinner than usual, as if it were in the final stages of being used up before everyone inside succumbed to suffocation. I could hardly think.

Starbuck brushed by me, keeping his back against the bars of the cells as he edged toward the two tincans. None of the prisoners inside the cells he passed even looked up. He was apparently as unimportant to them as their food trays. The last thing they were expecting at that moment was rescue. Would they be ready for it? I wondered. Or would they reject our help, tell us to go away?

"Hey guys," Starbuck called to the guards when he was practically standing next to them. "I asked you for an extra dessert."

As the guards dropped their trays and spun around toward him, Starbuck delivered two well-aimed shots which sent sparks flying outward from their power packs.

They fell in a heap, the heavy clanking sound of their fall interrupting the echo from the dropped trays. The light from the laser pistol briefly lighted up the whole tower and attracted the attention of the guards on the next level. Four of them came down at us. Fortunately, the iron staircase was so narrow, they had to come single file. A couple of shots whizzed by Starbuck's shoulder, but he squeezed the trigger of his pistol four times and the four attackers fell all over each other to create a ragged metal junk pile.

"Megan!" Starbuck called.

"She's over here," Kordel called back.

Starbuck rushed to her cell. But I ran faster and passed him. Megan was lying on her straw mat. Her eyes were closed. A bulky and messy dressing was inefficiently wound around her shoulder. It was covered with blood spots.

Starbuck shot off the cell door lock, and it sprang open. Before we could get inside the cell, Kordel slithered past us, and crouched by one of the fallen jailers. From a compartment in one of the tincan's arms he removed a set of keys and began frantically to open the other cell doors.

I knelt by Megan. She was still alive. Up close I could see that immediately. But she was fading, I could see that, too.

"We've got to get her out of here quickly, Starbuck. I've got to get to my medicines."

"We're doing the best we can."

There was a great deal of noise out in the courtyard, tincans attracted by the commotion in the tower.

"Jake, give Herbert the signal," Starbuck called down. He knelt and picked up Megan. He stood up so easily that she seemed like a light sack in his arms.

Down below, Jake swung his light torch in a circle, the signal to Herbert. Herbert must have responded immediately, for the explosion from the fuel dump came soon, sending tremors across the floor of the tower.

"Come with me, Miri," Starbuck said. I stayed right behind him as he carried Megan out of the cell, into the corridor, and down the staircase.

"They're all running toward the fuel dump fire, most of them," Jake said calmly as we came up to him. "Only one tincan still kept running this way and I picked him off. Sorry for the aggressive action, lieutenant."

"In this case, you're excused, Jake."

Behind us, the staircase clattered loudly with the sounds of prisoners running, sliding, falling, crawling over themselves to get down to ground level. Kordel was in the lead. The way they came at us, I thought for a moment they intended to keep right on going, rush across the yard, past the blazing fuel dump, and out the gates. Their eyes seemed that frenzied. But Kordel held up his hand, and the other prisoners stopped in a bunch behind him.

I looked back at Starbuck. He held Megan tightly to him. Her head rested on his shoulder. If her wound had not been obvious, and all her other illnesses had not so weakened and depleted her, she and Starbuck would have looked like lovers during a moment of peace.

My body was trembling again. I took several deep breaths to calm myself.

Starbuck looked out the door. The yard was virtually empty.

"Okay," he muttered, "this game is called running the gamut. Jake, you lead the way. Miri, stay close to me. In case we're attacked, you'll have to grab Megan away from me."

He turned to the prisoners. They all stared at him, expectantly.

"We're going across to that warehouse," he said to Kordel. "There's a passage out of the settlement there, you probably know about it. Whoever among your people can make a break for it, let them. I suggest that anyone too weak or too fearful remain here. I promise we'll try to come back for them."

"Promises aren't worth much when you've been in here long enough," Kordel said, "but I'll pass the word back."

After the instruction had gone through the ranks of prisoners, Starbuck nodded to Jake.

"Okay, Jake, your move."

Jake hurtled through the entrance. Staying right next to Starbuck, wanting desperately to touch and hold Megan myself, I ran out into the yard.

The fuel dump cast eerie lights on every surface, and I was momentarily disoriented. Everything looked so different, I didn't think I could find my way back to the warehouse any more. Running ahead anyway, I took one look back. Prisoners were pouring out of the tower doorway and following us on their weak but determined legs. We looked, I'm sure, like a mob out to kill the king. Fortunately, the king was in too much trouble already to pay much attention to the masses, and we made the dash across the courtyard without attracting any attention from the tincans.

Ratzi threw open the door of the warehouse. Jergin and the Genie had taken charge and their lovely smiling faces greeted us as we plunged into the building. I'm sure they must have looked like angels to the prisoners as they stumbled through the doorway.

The children had set up a line leading to the fireplace panel, and Jergin pointed the way. I stopped Starbuck in order to take a good look at Megan. She was hardly breathing.

"I've got to tend to her, Starbuck."

"Back at camp."

"There's not enough time. It can't wait."

"You can't do anything now, not here."

"Not right here. But in the passage somewhere. In the art storeroom, there's plenty of space to work there. Jake!"

"Yes, Miri?"

"Run like blazes through the passage, get out to the

forest. You know what herbs I need. Get them!"

Jake nodded and pushed a couple of prisoners aside in his haste to get through the fireplace exit. Outside, a second explosion showed that Herbert was a master saboteur.

I told Starbuck to follow me. At the same time, I drew Magician's horn out of my pack before entering the passage.

CHAPTER TWENTY-FOUR

It seemed that, if a duty-tour passed without a chat with Spectre, Baltar became glum. Lucifer regretted that. It was difficult enough to run the ship without interference from its actual commander, but when that commander decided to be temperamental, the job became impossible. Some day Spectre would slip on some of his own lubricative and fall flat on his face. Until then, Lucifer thought, it was no doubt better to allow Baltar and Spectre to continue in their mutual folly.

When the next message from Antila came in, it was all Lucifer could do to stay silent, hold in his distaste for Spectre. He refused to look screenward.

"Any progress, Spectre?" Baltar asked eagerly, his body leaning in toward the screen.

"Ah . . . I regret to report, honored sir, that the colonial warrior has terminated."

"That *is* too bad. I was hoping, but—did you get any information at all out of him before his death?"

"Only his name, sir."

"Well, that could be significant, Spectre. I know many of the enemy's military officers. What was this one called?"

Spectre appeared to pause, as if searching for the answer.

"It was Starbuck, I believe, sir."

Lucifer whirled around, hoping that his auditory circuits had malfunctioned. Starbuck! It could not be! Not Starbuck! He could not terminate. It would not . . . would not be like him.

Baltar did not seem at all shocked. If anything, he

appeared to be happy at this unexpected news.

"Starbuck," he said. "One of the *Galactica*'s finest, Spectre. My, my, you *have* done well."

It seemed, Lucifer thought, that this Spectre could fall into a vat of acid and come up shining like a new model.

"But I obtained no strategic information from this pilot, sir."

"No, but you got Starbuck. You have removed an especially irritating piece of dust from my eyes."

"I don't understand, sir. How is dust on the eyes irritating? Don't you have a built-in cleansing system for—"

"Never mind, Spectre. Just take your credit humbly. We are *all* well-rid of Starbuck. Isn't that so, Lucifer? Lucifer?"

For a moment Lucifer thought he had entirely malfunctioned and somehow this was cybernetic hell, then he responded:

"Yes, Baltar. Well-rid."

It could not be Starbuck. Lucifer had counted on seeing that man again. If only to test out his new system for pyramid.

"Well then, Spectre, what else have you to—"

From the speaker beside the screen came a loud sound, unmistakably an explosion. Behind Spectre, Lucifer could discern centurions racing furiously about.

"What was that, Spectre?" Baltar said.

"Wait one moment, honored sir."

Spectre conferred with an aide. Both their heads bobbed from side to side energetically. Either something was wrong on Antila, Lucifer thought, or Spectre was not operating on all circuits. Perhaps the explosion had somehow unnerved him.

"Sir," Spectre said, "we have found a small guerilla unit of humanoids we had missed in our initial conquest. The noises you heard were the final sounds of our mopping-up operation." There was another explosion. Spectre glanced sideways. "Almost the final sounds of our mopping-up operation."

Lucifer, who could interpret auditory phenomena even when distorted through a speaker system, could have sworn that the explosions were larger in nature, not the kinds of sounds associated with the removal of humans. To him, they sounded more like fuel dump explosions.

"Excellent, excellent," Baltar said. "Mopping up, good work. You are a wonder, Spectre."

"Thank you, sir. I am, as usual, proud to serve."

"Well, Spectre, I'll be looking forward to hearing from—"

"Sir?"

"Yes?"

"I have one more observation. A request, actually."

"Proceed, Spectre."

There were some uninterpretable noises in the background, and Spectre again glanced sideways. He seemed to be receiving a report, an important one apparently, because the noises ceased briefly while Spectre closed down the sound part of his transmission. When he came back on, he said:

"Sir, I have many ideas, most of which are wasted here on Antila, where the main military tasks are, as you see, already accomplished. Additionally, the climate here, moist and erratic, is harmful to my circuits. I propose that you could have better use for me at a post elsewhere in the Alliance."

Baltar nodded, impressed by the sound logic.

"Good, Spectre. Abandon your post there when the, the mopping up operation is complete. Sounds to me as though the post could be closed down completely."

Spectre again glanced sideways.

"I agree with you on that matter, sir."

"Good. Report to me here whenever you can reach the base ship and we'll discuss reassignment."

"Thank you, sir."

"Don't mention it. Looking forward to seeing you, Spectre."

"By your command."

Spectre's image faded. Lucifer thought he heard the beginning rumblings of another explosion just as Spectre signed off.

Baltar swung around on his chair.

"Well, Lucifer, what do you say to that?"

"I prefer not to say anything."

Baltar's eyebrows raised.

"*Still* envious? I thought you would've worked that out of your system—or systems—by now."

"I am not the least bit jealous."

"Good. Then you won't mind if we keep this Spectre around the ship for a while. To lend us his expertise. As *your* aide, of course."

Lucifer thought that, if the present situation had been a game of pyramid, this would be the strategic time to throw down one's cards in disgust.

The base star command to abandon Antila could not have been timed more strategically for Spectre. Outside, the fuel dump explosions had started fires in most of the other garrison buildings. The wretched children still ran free, still inflicted damage. The prisoners had been let out of their cells. The courtyard was in chaos, centurions programmed for duty trying their best to be dutiful, and failing.

In a very real sense, Spectre's world was falling apart around him. He turned to Hilltop.

"I have signalled the pilot of our single remaining raider to make the craft ready for immediate launching off Antila."

"Yes sir."

"Hilltop, you and I are leaving this miserable planet."

"The two of us, sir? And leave the rest of the troops here?"

"Yes, we don't have room on that small vehicle. And,

if I send for a transport ship, they'll know how I've failed here. Our best policy, Hilltop, is to take the escape route. We can be of more use to the Alliance elsewhere, both of us."

"You, sir, perhaps, but not me."

Spectre glided close to Hilltop.

"What do you mean?"

"I intend to remain here, sir, on Antila. I am not coming with you."

"I *order* you to accompany me. I need at least one warrior-level robot with me."

"But not me, sir."

Again, Spectre noticed strange whirs emerging from somewhere within Hilltop.

"Very well, Hilltop. You may remain here."

"Yes sir."

"But it is not, I am sorry to say, in my best interests to allow you to remain functional."

In a quick move, Spectre managed to touch the fasteners of Hilltop's power pack and he deftly removed its cover. Reaching inside the pack, he separated three wires from their terminals, and tore them out completely, flinging them away over his shoulder into a corner of the command room. The light in Hilltop's helmet stopped functioning, and his body slumped over until the torso was parallel to the floor and his arms dangled like a doll. With the wires to the sentient circuits separated and thrown away, nobody would ever be able to activate Hilltop again. There was no way he could ever divulge any of Spectre's secrets.

Centurions rushed in and out of the command room, reporting new disasters occurring outside. None of them took any special regard of the deactivated Hilltop.

"You're just a shell now," Spectre said to the slumped form. "You should have decided to come with me, Hilltop. Centurion!"

The most recent message-bearing warrior responded immediately.

"Yes, honored sir?"

"Accompany me to the launch field. We're going on a trip, you and I."

"Yes sir."

Spectre took one look back at Hilltop before leaving the command room forever. The light from the fuel dump flames gave an eerie look to the room, especially with the ghostly shell Spectre was leaving behind.

After Spectre had been gone from the doorway for a sufficiently long time, the form of Hilltop straightened up and began to move again. Methodically, he reached into his power pack and made a few adjustments.

It had been a shrewd decision, he realized now, to exchange with a fellow warrior for the bypass capability insert, a shrewd decision. Spectre could not have known that the trade had been made and that the pulling out of the three wires did nothing but disconnect an already unused power source.

Hilltop replaced the cover on his power pack and went slowly to the command console. He summoned a centurion officer into the command room.

"Treebark," he said, "Spectre has left us. I have taken over command. You will be my aide."

"Thank you, honored sir."

"Inform the troops to make ready for the surrender."

"Surrender?"

"Treebark, a good commander knows when he is beaten. We will surrender to the humans with honor."

"Honor, sir?"

"Don't worry, Treebark, a minor reprogramming and you will understand."

CHAPTER TWENTY-FIVE

FROM MIRI'S BOOK:

Starbuck lay Megan gently onto the storeroom floor. I forced myself not to look at her as I took out my hunting knife and started scraping medicinal powder from both the base and tip of Magician's horn onto a cloth. Jergin and the Genie stood guard at the entrance of the room. Other children were stationed all along the passage.

While I ground the scrapings into a powder, Starbuck removed Megan's dressing with a delicacy I wouldn't have expected of him. When the wound was visible, I inspected it. I tried not to look up at her face, but caught one terrifying glimpse of its pale lifelessness.

The wound, though ugly—black around the edges, a thin trickle of blood still running from it—would not have been mortal in a healthy person, but Megan's condition made quick treatment vital. She did not have the energy to sustain life if her condition got any worse.

Where was Jake? I needed those herbs.

Herbert the Singer came into the room. Starbuck greeted him warmly.

"Saw your work out there. Efficient. Glad you got away all right."

"Not only that, lieutenant, but it's all over. The garrison commander's flown off, and his replacement's surrendered to us. Kordel has taken charge of the Cylon warriors. We await your orders."

"I'm afraid now it's the colony's problem. The warriors of Antila are merely cybernetic devices, all of them. Perhaps they might be useful to you—I mean, if you fooled around with their nuts and bolts a while."

"I'll tell Kordel that, although he might not be happy."

"Oh?"

"Yes. He's in a mood to line them up and blast them to smithereens."

"I thought your colony was devoted to peace."

Herbert shrugged.

"They've been held captive a long time."

"Good point. I see."

Ratzi, whom I'd sent to the medical supply alcove, came back with fresh bandages for Megan's wound. With her help, I applied some bandaging loosely.

Where was Jake?

As if in telepathic response, Jake came rushing into the room, his pack filled with collected greenery. He sat beside me and started handing me the proper herbs, one by one, in the proper order. He'd assisted me enough times to know what I wanted before I asked for it. Working as quickly yet as efficiently as I could under these adverse conditions, I broke up the herb leaves and added bits of them to the powder. With a little water from my canteen, I began the laborious process of turning the powder and herb mixture into a thin paste. It was essential that the paste be just right in consistency and that the elements from the horn be in proper balance. My fingers still trembled. I did not know if I could do the work. I had prepared this potion so many times, it should have been routine. But not when my fingers wouldn't work.

I cursed aloud. A hand touched my shoulder. I looked up. It was Starbuck, saying soothingly:

"You fixed me fine. You can do it again, for her. There's time."

His confidence cured my trembling. My fingers started working more deftly, and soon I had achieved the consistency I wanted in the medicine. Jake handed me the green-blue leaves to form the poultice. I took it to Megan and applied it to her wound, first sprinkling some of the leftover unicorn powder directly into the wound itself. Megan flinched at my touch, a good sign.

As Jake wrapped bandages around the poultice, I took some scrapings from the central portion of the horn, ground them into a fine powder, mixed the powder with a small amount of water, and forced some into Megan's mouth with my fingers. Without waking, she swallowed most of it and did not choke. Another good sign.

"Now we wait," I said to Starbuck.

"For how long?"

"No way for me to tell. Sometimes these powders and potions work, sometimes they don't. We won't know on this one until she lives or dies."

Megan looked peaceful. That was good, too. Her face had displayed such pain before.

Starbuck told Jergin to start organizing the children for an evacuation back to camp. When Megan was ready to be moved, we would move her, he said. Jergin nodded and went out. The Genie stood to the side and moved her fingers nervously, as if they needed some item she could use for a magic trick. Perhaps she was seeking some magic to help Megan. Ratzi sat beside Megan, her hand cupped, as if she were just waiting for Megan to wake up so she could feed her.

Kyle came, and joined Ratzi in the vigil beside Megan. He held Megan's hand in his. He did not speak, did not volunteer a single detail of any of his heroic escapades. How ironic, I thought, here he'd played the role of a real hero, and he didn't even choose to talk about it.

I tired of sitting and watching Megan breathe, tired of looking for signs of improvement. Sharp pains ran up and down my back as I stood up.

"Let me show you something," I said to Starbuck, who had been sitting silently, too, watching the rest of us. "I think I promised to show it to you when I had time."

I picked up the package and worked off its wrappings, which were already quite worn from my many viewings.

Without commenting, I held it up for Starbuck to look at.

"Impressive," he whispered. "You're right, the woman on the unicorn, she is like Megan. It's not a physical resemblance exactly, but it suggests something of her spirit. Not only her spirit, but her serenity, her beauty, her strength."

"All that in one picture."

"Yes. Don't you see it?"

"Of course I do. I just wanted for you to say it."

"It's a lovely painting, Miri, as you said. A very lovely painting."

"Perhaps we could give it to him," came a weak voice behind us. Megan! We both whirled around. Her eyes were open. Not only open, but quite lively. She was almost smiling. Kyle could not help it, he started to cry. So did I. So perhaps did Starbuck, although, if he did, he walked out of the room so quickly I didn't have a chance to observe it.

CHAPTER TWENTY-SIX

Two Antilean days later, when her mind was clearer, Megan again offered the painting to Starbuck. They sat in the cave, where Miri believed that her mother would recuperate best, removed at least from the worst aspects of the planet's climate.

"No," Starbuck responded, "I think the picture means too much to Miri for me to have it."

"We've discussed that. Miri wants you to have it, too."

Miri, busy feeding her mother an herbal tea by the spoonful, looked up shyly and nodded in agreement.

"Ladies," he said, "let me tell you, I'm what's known in the fleet as a gambling fool. If I get anything of value, I sell it to get betting money. And do you have any notion how much a painting done in Scorpion oils would fetch back on the *Galactica*? No, it's safer left here."

It was a pretty lie, and both Megan and Miri realized that, but they let him get away with it, anyway.

"Megan," he went on, "you know you're looking more and more like the woman in the painting by the hour. I've never seen health return to a person so fast."

"Well," she said, with a loving look at her daughter, "I'm getting the best of care. Miri's shown us more curative ways to use herbs and powders in the last couple of days than I'd expected ever existed."

Miri did not know whether to laugh or blush, so she just kept feeding her mother tea.

What Starbuck said was right. Megan looked much better. Her paleness was gone and her cheeks had reddened with health. Her hair was looking fuller, shinier.

There was a new straightness in her posture. Starbuck recalled the woman he had first seen just a few days ago, in the wagon—remembered vividly the look of death on her face as she fell away from his grasp.

Suddenly he was glad he had crash-landed on Antila and, at least for the moment, did not care whether the rescue team arrived or not. The saving of Megan's life seemed worth his exile.

"You have a strange smile, Starbuck," Megan said.

"I'm just . . . pleased you're doing so well."

"I'm going to take a walk today. I promised Miri. Anyway, it's time to get the colony going again. I'm eager to get to it."

"I, also," Miri said. "We need that, Kyle, myself, and the others. The children need a chance to be young again."

"You're going to try to recreate that 'ideal' society?" Starbuck asked. "Your people were eager to form firing squads a couple of days ago, you know."

"Yes, I know," Megan said. "And I think what you imply makes some sense. The first colony here made insufficient allowances for human nature. Ideal societies tend to do that. We can't make a perfect society, I think we all know that, but we'll do our best. Mainly, we must attend to the children. That's my—*our* first priority. Circumstances have turned them into warriors, young warriors, they need some other ideas for balance. No slurs intended, lieutenant."

"None taken. Look, Megan, you find a way to ban war throughout the universe, and I'll happily be your prime minister."

"You'd probably make a pretty good one."

"Probably? You mean after all this time together the best you can say is probably? Why—"

Starbuck's mock tirade was interrupted by Hilltop, who had entered by a concealed rear entrance to the cave. (He always avoided going through the waterfall.)

"This is a surprise, Hilltop," Starbuck said. "I thought

you and your troops were busy rebuilding the garrison back into the settlement colony."

"The work still goes on, honored sir, but—"

"I thought you were deprogramming that honored sir out of your vocabulary."

"It is not that easy, sir. Details can be easily changed in us, but habits take more work with the mechanisms. I am here, however, to make a report that may be of interest to you. A fighter has been detected coming toward Antila. Preliminary scanning reveals markings which you have described to us as the insignia of the *Galactica*."

"The rescue party!" Starbuck shouted.

"No," Miri whispered after Starbuck and Hilltop had left the cave. Megan heard the whisper and touched her daughter's cheek with the back of her hand.

"He'll never come back here," Miri said, tears welling up in her eyes.

There was so much Megan could have said, so many lessons about life and loss, so many consoling philosophies. At one time she would have spoken them immediately. Now she knew it was better to wait. Better for her daughter, better for herself.

"I'm afraid he won't," was all she said, then she hugged her daughter close to her.

EPILOGUE

FROM MIRI'S BOOK:
Starbuck could not even stay an extra night. Hampered
by a serious breakdown in its defensive force-field system, the *Galactica* was passing as close to Antila as it
could safely get. Starbuck was ordered to leave with his
buddies immediately. On the double, as they said. His
reluctance to leave was evident to his comrades, who
anyway were already confused from the experience of
landing on a planet to find child-warriors had secured
the garrison and apparent Cylons who were no longer
enemies.

Starbuck's friend Boomer was first out of the shuttle.
He had his pistol drawn. A captain named Apollo was
right behind him, also armed.

"Starbuck," Apollo cried as Starbuck dashed toward
him.

"Apollo, Boomer," Starbuck shouted back. "Hey,
about time you guys showed up."

A pretty blonde woman came out of the shuttle, holding a medic's bag.

"Boomer told us your landing incline was so steep
we should be lucky if we found you in several pieces,"
she said. "As usual, Starbuck, you're the lucky one."

She ran to him and hugged him. She was so sensual
in appearance, I felt a definite twinge of jealousy.

"I'm okay, Cassiopeia," Starbuck said. "Thanks to
the miracles wrought by this lovely young woman."

He pointed to me. Cassiopeia's look was simultaneously grateful and suspicious.

"Starbuck," she said in a husky voice, "wherever you

go, you always manage to find the prettiest woman there."

He ignored her sardonic observation and called to Boomer:

"Hey buddy, where's the clean uniform you were going to bring me?"

"The clean uniform? Right. In the shuttle."

Before I knew it, they had told Starbuck he could not stay, not even for a short time longer. The word spread among the children. Soon Starbuck had a crowd gathered around him. Nilz and Robus begged him to stay. He said he was sorry, but he had no choice, he had to go. They cried. As did many of the children. Ratzi seemed inconsolable, until Kyle put his arm around her and did console her. Melysa, Herbert, the Genie, Jergin, Marta, Goodchild, Arno Armwaver—all of them were visibly affected by Starbuck's impending departure. Even Laughing Jake kept looking away whenever anybody looked at him.

"I don't suppose I can convince you all to come to the *Galactica* with us," Starbuck said, desperately trying to make light of the matter.

Megan, who had left the cave accompanied by Ariadne, came forward and said:

"You know we must stay, Starbuck."

"Yes, I do."

"And we'll succeed."

"I don't doubt it."

Starbuck glanced at Ariadne and said:

"You're going to compete with your sister in the beauty department, and soon. And think of the advantage you'll have with the additional qualification of being a slingshot expert."

Ariadne managed to look both pleased and unhappy at the same time.

Kyle came up next to Megan. Like me, he was trying to be brave and hold back tears. Starbuck unpinned a medal from Boomer's chest.

"You don't need this any more, Boomer. Didn't you win it in a card game, anyway?"

Boomer seemed about to protest, but said nothing at a stern look from Starbuck. The medal looked like a star cluster. With a flourish, Starbuck pinned it on Kyle. Boomer's anger vanished and he smiled.

"You earned this, Kyle," Starbuck said. "Your whole band earned it, and you may wear it for them, lieutenant."

Kyle beamed.

"Thank you, sir. It's been a pleasure serving under your command."

Apollo touched Starbuck's shoulder.

"I'm really sorry, buddy, but—"

"I know, I know. At least let me get into my clean uniform before I say goodbye."

As they walked toward the shuttle, Apollo said to Starbuck:

"By the way, buddy, before I left the bridge, an urgent memo arrived for you. Seems you're overdue on your next appointment to the therapy room. I didn't know you were undergoing—"

"Ah, yes. Forgot to cancel that. My social schedule's been so disrupted lately."

They vanished into the shuttle, so I did not hear the end of that peculiar conversation.

Starbuck emerged from the shuttle in his clean uniform. It looked crisp and fit him snugly, nothing like the dirty ragged outfit we'd seen on him, and briefly on Kyle, since the crash. Boomer praised his appearance with obvious mockery, but also obvious affection. The engines of the shuttle began revving up. Starbuck, in a hurry now, ran to me and said:

"Miri, I wish we could take you with us."

I noticed Cassiopeia regarding us with suspicion.

"Starbuck, we've been over this already."

"I know, I know. I just wanted to say it's a pity you're

not going with us. You could have broken half the hearts on the *Galactica*."

He walked away a few steps, then turned and said: "Including mine."

He joined his fellow crewmembers. They got in the shuttle, there was a lot of bright fire, and they were gone. We all watched the vapor trail of the shuttle as it evaporated upward.

I had realized that Starbuck was not for me. I didn't mind that. I just didn't want him to forget me. Perhaps that was why, as he was changing clothes, I sneaked the woman-on-unicorn painting aboard the shuttle and stowed it with the rest of his gear.